OVER RAINBOWS

Marie Osburn Reid

Happy reading
Marie Osburn Reid

Amazon Breakthrough Novel Award Reviews:

I really liked this piece. It was simply written without being too dramatic or over generalized.

This is an exciting tale of two young sisters travelling by ship in the 1920's to Alaska with intriguing characters, plot and setting.

The story promises to be a fairly engaging account of how two plucky sisters are going to make their way in the rugged world of Alaska Territory. And, of course, there is the whole question of if and why someone may want them dead.

Publisher Weekly: An unusual setting and strong, clear prose enliven this juvenile mystery.

CONTENTS

ACKNOWLEDGMENTS

The book cover is taken from a portion of stained glass dedicated to the memory of Bishop Bill Gordon known as 'Alaska's flying bishop'. The window is at St. Matthew's Church in Fairbanks, Alaska. The talented artist is Debbie Mathews, proprietor of a lovely shop and gallery named Expressions in Glass.

An acknowledgement of sincere appreciation for editing expertise goes to Carla Helfferich, and to my helpful husband, Reford (Jeep) Reid. A big thanks for reviews by many readers on Fan Story.

CHAPTER 1

Sail from Seattle

"Alaska. Here we come!" I shouted above squawking seabirds on Seattle's Pier 67.

With my fists planted on the waist of my navy-blue sailor dress, I relished the sight of a majestic steamship, the *Northwestern*. Bright morning sunshine glistened off the ship's three white decks that towered above its expansive black-painted sides.

My sister, Julianne, hastened out on the pier. A kid-gloved hand pressed on my shoulder in a way too rigid to be reassuring. My steady, confident sister looked fashionable in her lime-green dress and flapper hat. However her voice came with a shaky breath when she sighed, "Well, Tish, it looks sturdy enough to take us to Alaska."

"Matisha," scolded Mr. Sundborg, our attorney. I had earned his disapproval by bolting from his fancy, new Model T Ford. "It behooves young ladies to observe proper etiquette and allow a gentleman to open the doors of an automobile properly. I hope this demonstration of poor manners is not indicative of future behavior as you travel on your own."

"We appreciate all the trouble you've gone to for us." My sister's reply was barely audible above the screeches of seagulls.

Mr. Sundborg peered over his spectacles at Julianne. "I must repeat my objection to your traveling without an escort. You are not even twenty yet, and caring for your little sister is a big responsibility for a young lady. Besides, it is not proper."

My cheeks burned at being called 'little'. "I am exactly twelve and a half."

Mr. Sundborg snatched a carpetbag and tossed it at me. I caught it with a thud against my chest. My long braids jumped over my shoulders.

"Times are changing," Julianne said. Her pretty green eyes blinked with uncertainty at the number of men crowding aboard the ship. She cleared her throat. "We'll manage just fine on our own, Mr. Sundborg."

"This is the Roaring 20's," I spouted. A soft white glove with iron fingers inside squeezed my arm. I twisted free of my sister, but swallowed away philosophical thoughts that burned in my brain.

The attorney hesitated. His teeth were clenched. "Mind you, keep your distance from all those men traveling without wives." He strode up to the purser, took papers from his vest pocket and showed him our boarding passes. "Have a porter fetch Miss Dushan's trunk next, won't you?"

The purser nodded to a nearby seaman, who quickly lifted the trunk from the car and tossed it carelessly atop the pile on a cart. As he trudged up the gangplank, I hustled after him. Julianne trailed us with Mr. Sundborg.

"There is really no need for you to see us aboard, Mr. Sundborg," Julianne told him.

"Now, I'm a thorough man when it comes to keeping a promise. Jonah P. Dushan rests peacefully knowing his children are launched on their way to a secure future in Alaska."

Hearing Papa's name stopped me like a spider trapped under glass. I turned around to see Julianne gazing at scant clouds in the blue morning sky. Her jaw was rigid, holding back either words or tears. Both of us knew that we really did owe a lot to this irritating man. We had counted on him during those long months when Papa was so sick. He was our guardian and, because of him, Papa's plan for us was right on course. For that I was glad. Yet, I wished a giant hand would swoop down and carry the attorney back into the city. Such impatience gave me pangs of guilt, made me feel disloyal to Papa.

"Your father knew what was best for you." Mr. Sundborg rested against the railing to catch his breath before resuming his march up the incline of the gangplank. "An upstanding citizen like Mr. Lewiston Kelovich is a fine match."

Julianne's face momentarily blanched. "Thank you for all your help. Please consider your duty done, Mr. Sundborg." She planted an impulsive kiss on his cheek.

"Well," he stammered, obviously stunned by her pretty, soft lips on his skin. "I dare say I do believe you will manage as well as can be expected from here on in."

I mustered all the politeness I could and crossed my arms. "Goodbye, Mr. Sundborg, and thank you."

He tipped his derby hat and backed away. "Good luck in Alaska, my dears."

I stepped up onto our trunk to see him get away through the crowd. "Yuck! I'm glad he didn't expect me to kiss him."

She winked at me and half smiled.

I saw him step off the gangplank and climb into the Ford. With sweet relief, I surveyed all the people on the dock. A woman holding a baby caught my eye. She gave her husband a goodbye hug while a small boy clung to his father's pant leg.

"How sad, that little boy doesn't want his father to go." My eyes went watery.

"I remember the feeling. When I was little I used to beg Papa not to leave us," Julianne said.

"It's when he finally came home from the gold rush that I felt bad. I didn't even know him."

"You were only five then." Julianne pulled me against her in a tender hug. "Let's be thankful he was with us when we needed him most, after Mama got so terribly sick."

I let out the thought that had danced in my head for weeks."Papa would be proud of us going to Alaska just like he did."

"I'm sure he would." Julianne frowned. "Going to Alaska is an adventure, but we're also leaving behind everything we've ever known."

My stomach did a flip-flop until I spotted a rainbow. Its colors blazed to the north. "Look." I pointed at the sky. "It's a good omen. We're sailing toward that beautiful rainbow."

We gazed skyward for a moment, then turned and were face-to-face with a suntanned seaman. He stopped right in front of us.

"Pardon me, could you be the Dushan sisters?" He asked with a friendly grin. Sun-bleached curls escaped from his knit cap.

"That's us," I replied. "This is our first time on a ship. Are you a sailor?"

"I am Daniel O'Keefe at your service." He bent in a slight bow. "A friend inquired if you had boarded."

"We know no one who could be a passenger," Julianne said.

"Did he have spectacles and a black derby over an almost bald head?" I was certain Mr. Sundborg was checking up on us already.

"No. He definitely is a sourdough type. Rumpled and the worse for wear, if you don't mind my saying."

"We don't know anyone like that," I exclaimed.

"I'm sure there's some mistake." Julianne said.

The sailor's eyes widened. He scratched the knit hat on his head. His confused look gave me goose-bumps.

CHAPTER 2

Meet Alice

Julianne shrugged off his look of surprise. "Mr. O'Keefe, would you point our way to number 22 stateroom?"

"I'll be happy to show you where you'll be bunking." The sailor hoisted our trunk to his shoulder with ease. "It ain't no stateroom, though it'll keep you out of the weather."

"That's good enough," I said with thoughts about our home in Seattle. It was in an apartment house. The halls smelled of dinner cooking from twelve different kitchens. Julianne and I shared a bedroom. There was Papa's bedroom, a sitting room with gas lights, and running water in the kitchen and bathroom.

Daniel O'Keefe tilted his clean-shaven chin toward the ship's bow. "Follow me, ladies."

He led us through a maze of passengers and baggage piled on the deck. Up a flight of stairs, I had to drag my carpetbag one step at a time. On the second deck, a long row of doors faced the ship's guardrail. Each door was labeled with a brass number.

At door 22 he asked, "You two rooming alone?"

"Oh no, that would be too costly," Julianne said. "I don't know who is to be with us."

The door burst open and a bright-eyed, a tad plump young woman appeared.

"It will be me, Alice Allen." She had heard us through the thin door. "You must be Julianne, and you must be Matisha from Seattle on your way to Fairbanks, the same as me. They told me at the registrar. I just couldn't wait to know."

"That's us. But you can call me Tish," I said, and gazed at a pretty, round face with rosy cheeks and lush blond hair cut in the latest bob.

"Pleased to meet you," Julianne said. "And this helpful man is Daniel...."

"Dan O'Keefe." He grinned. "I'm sailing out of Frisco on my third time north."

"Well, do set that heavy trunk down before your shoulder breaks." Alice fluttered soft eyelashes at him.

With a grunt he set the trunk just inside the door.

"Thank you for the help, Daniel." Julianne reaches a gloved hand for him to take. He lightly holds it but dropped it, slightly startled when Alice speaks.

"I hope you'll come by and help again when we get to Seward." Alice's face glowed with a coquettish smile.

Daniel's oversized ears burned red. "Well, Captain Hale will cast off real soon now. I'll see you ladies about the ship, maybe often."

"Bye, Dan," we called as he walked away.

Alice gazed after him. "Good looking, don't you think?"

"He's really strong," I said and swallowed a giggle. My eyes met Julianne's and I could see she was thinking the same as me. Mr. Sundborg would not approve of the way Alice flirted with the sailor.

The cabin was so small that all three of us could not stand at once and still maneuver. I looked around and cried, "Dibs on the top bunk!"

"Fine with me." Alice had belongings strung across a single bed with cupboards overhead. She ducked her head and settled onto the narrow bed.

There was room to store the trunk under the bunks. With a grunt, I helped Julianne shove it into place. I took Raggedy Ann from my bag and climbed up the bunk ladder. I pressed wrinkles out of my ragdoll's special dress. Even though I gave up playing with dolls long ago, this one had been sewn by my mother. Raggedy Ann belonged to what was left of our family.

Julianne hung her cape on a coat-hook by the door. Alice looked her over. "Nice drop-waist dress. So fashionable with the rope of pearls."

"Thank you, Alice." Julianne pulled off her flapper cap. Glossy, deep auburn curls fell about her shoulders.

"Oh, such long hair. You had me fooled, Julianne." Alice touched her own short, blonde waves.

"Look at these pigtails. I just hate them, but I love your short bob, Alice. I wish I could get my hair bobbed."

"I will gladly cut it for you, Tish. I just graduated from the Tacoma School of Hair Styling and Cosmetology. That's why I didn't go with my parents and little brother to Alaska last fall."

"Is it okay, Julianne? May Alice cut my hair?"

"You know Papa would not have approved, Tish."

I grabbed my braids, tied them under my chin and stuck out my tongue.

"Such a clown." Alice said with a laugh.

Julianne wagged her head.

"Please." I clasped my pleading hands together.

"I really do need the practice," my new best friend said.

Julianne heaved a sigh. "I leave it up to you, Tish."

"Hooray, tell me when, Alice. I can hardly wait."

Julianne rolled her eyes at me then turned to Alice. "I think it's terrific you have a career." They both began to pull under things from carpetbags and place them neatly in two small drawers.

"That's what my mother says, but Father has less progressive ideas about a woman's place. He's the grocery and dry goods manager for the Alaska Commercial Company. He only hires women when he can find no good men."

"And the women are paid half as much, right?"

"No doubt about that."

"When you have your own beauty shop, you should hire only women," I said.

"My own shop? The thought takes my breath away. Do I dare hope enough women could want my services?"

"Men need haircuts." I held up Raggedy Ann and combed my fingers through the yarn her head.

"There should be no reason why a barber has to be a man," Julianne said.

Alice's eyes twinkled. "They say there are heaps of men in Fairbanks, the unattached kind. The ratio is all in our favor."

"It's not a man in Alaska that my sister is interested in getting married to." I glare at Julianne.

Alice stopped folding a petticoat. She looked at Julianne with her mouth wide open."But surely you want to meet some wonderful guy sometime and get married. Don't you?"

"Julianne can marry the most wonderful man there if she just will."

Julianne sat down on her bunk and pulled her feet up to give Alice more floor space. "My first order of business in Fairbanks will be to figure out how not to get married."

"You mean you have a man waiting for you?"

"Oh yes, she sure does."

"How incredibly thrilling!"

"I'll show you." I rummaged through my bag until my hand touched the photograph. "Exactly to this handsome man."

Alice stared at a man posed with one foot on the carcass of a huge bear and leaning proudly on the butt of a rifle. "Oh, he looks quite remarkable. Why wouldn't you want to marry a man like that, Julianne?"

"Mainly, because I don't know him. The last time Lucky Lew was in Seattle I was younger than Tish."

"If you marry him then you won't be an old maid. We know he's super, Alice. Papa told us lots of stories about the fabulous Lucky Lew.

They were partners in the gold rush." I wanted Alice to be my new best friend for more reasons than my hair.

"Gracious, he sounds absolutely magnificent. But, wouldn't he be quite a bit older?"

"Old enough to be my father." Julianne sighed.

"But Papa really wanted you to marry him, Julianne. It was his dying wish." A lump stuck in my throat. My sister had heard all this from me before. It wasn't fair of me to say it right in front of Alice, but maybe, just maybe, it could make a difference.

"I know a woman who has a very happy marriage with an older man. And, this man is surely handsome and brave looking, and....."

Julianne interrupted Alice's anxious patter and gave me a can't-believe-you-said-that look. "Before our father died, he arranged this marriage for me. It was the way things were done when he was growing up in the old country. Our mother sailed from Europe when she was seventeen to become his bride. He had never laid eyes on her before she got off the boat. Arranged marriages are common to this day in Serbia."

"Well, this is America. Didn't he understand that things are different here?" Still holding the picture, Alice sat down beside Julianne.

I hugged Raggedy Ann. "When Papa was so sick, he wasn't afraid about dying. But he was afraid about leaving us alone in the world with no one to take care of us."

"Our mother passed away when Tish was just six," Julianne explained.

"Oh, Julianne, in that case...I mean...then maybe he was right." Alice's eyes glistened with tears. She gazed at the photo. "Maybe you should marry this great-looking and I'm sure a wonderful man."

"That's what I keep telling her."

"Hogwash! I'm sure I can make it on my own, especially in Alaska. Our father told us how independent women can be there."

"Really? How can that be?" A sideways grin made Alice look skeptical.

"Papa knew a woman who was a photographer, another who ran her own restaurant, and another who wrote articles for the newspaper. You see, I don't have to marry a breadwinner. I know I can support both of us. We're free to try out new things, Alice. And you really can start your very own barber shop!"

Alice dropped the Lucky Lew photo. "Julianne, you make my head spin."

My lower lip jutted out. "I think she should marry Lucky Lew."

The ship's whistle blew, piercing through the muffled noises of warming engines and passengers shuffling about the deck. We looked at each other and smiled with the same thought.

"Let's wave goodbye to Seattle." I scoot down off the bunk.

Alice squealed. "We're Territory bound at last!"

We rushed out. The guardrail was lined with passengers. Several men were politely quick to offer us space at the rail.

Alice waved madly to a plump woman in an old fashioned brimmed hat. The stern man beside her raised a hand as if he was doing a soldier's salute. "There's my Aunt Bertha and Uncle Edwin. They're still here waiting to see me gone. I'm going to miss Aunt Bertha."

No one was there to see Julianne and me off. The spot where Homer Sundborg's Ford had stood was empty. Our aunts or uncles lived on another continent. I turned away from the rail and saw the rainbow above the northern forest. Stripes of rose, green and yellow arched up from the city. I turned to tell Julianne that I predict we would find a pot of gold in the far north, but stopped when someone on the third deck above caught my eye.

A passenger in a rumpled coat was staring down at us. A slouched hat shaded most of his face. As he melted away into the crowd, I thought I saw a grin crease thin lips. Remembering how Dan O'Keefe described *a sourdough* made hair prickle at the back of my neck.

CHAPTER 3

Sea Legs and Seasick

As the ship moved slowly away from the dock and out into the bay, I pushed away the image of the creepy man. I chalked up the whole scene to too much imagination. I've been accused of that before.

"Look how all the houses are getting little," I called to Julianne and Alice. The smells of coal furnaces, horses and motorcars faded quickly. I breathed in only the fresh scent of the sea. At the edge of the wide, choppy water were lush, green hills and Mt. Rainier stood tall off in the distance with a sprinkle of snow not yet melted.

Alice stretched her arms to the panoramic scene of the Port of Seattle, Bainbridge Island and out to the end of Elliott Bay. "Let's always remember it just like this, like a beautiful painting."

Julianne stared back at the city with a gaze that told me she felt fearful and unsure of our future. I felt duty-bound to cheer her up so I suggested, "Let's explore the ship."

"Oh yes, let's start with the bow," Alice chimed with such bright-eyed anticipation that I had to giggle. Julianne smiled too. After many weeks of sadness that we shared, Alice's high spirit was refreshing.

As we strolled toward the front of the ship, I couldn't help comparing Alice to my sister. Julianne was reserved, totally ladylike and proper. Alice showed not a drop of caution. She smiled sweetly to people passing by, who were nearly all men.

Real soon, four young men walked with us eager to answer questions that Alice did not hesitate to ask. They explained the ship was 300 feet long, equipped with lifeboats, deck chairs, a galley and dining hall. When offers came to escort us to the dining hall to buy us coffee, Julianne firmly declined.

Back in our cabin, Julianne gently said, "Alice, you were flirting with those men. At that rate, we'll be in very hot water at the end of ten days."

"I thought they were nice," I said. Right or wrong, it was fun to watch Alice flirt.

"I promise to be more careful. But that tall

one with the dark eyes was really handsome, don't you think?"

"I can't think of which man you mean." I decided more than one was tall.

"Tish, cover your ears." Julianne laughed as she had not for a long, long time. "You are dizzy, Alice."

At the end of the day we discovered the food in the dining hall was good and hearty. The week's menu was posted on a chalkboard. Evenings, the cuisine would be meat, boiled vegetables, potatoes and gravy. Lunchtime offered all the soup and sandwiches we wanted, plus pie or cake would be available for late night snacking.

At our first breakfast, the scent of bacon and flapjacks filled the dining hall air. I had just poured on maple syrup when the seaman Daniel O'Keefe stopped by our table.

"Hello ladies." He tilted his curly head in a polite bow. "Miss Dushan, did your sourdough friend ever locate you?"

"The man you mentioned when we boarded?"

Goosebumps crept over my skin again. I snapped, "We don't know any man like that on this ship."

"Well, that's a surprise. I mean, that he hasn't found you yet. He said I should tell you he was looking for you."

Julianne frowned. "What an odd thing to say."

"Could he be a secret admirer, Julianne?" Alice smiled.

Julianne ignored her remark. "There's surely some mistake. Did he tell you his name, Daniel?"

"Nope. When I asked, he just grinned and walked away."

As soon as he said that about a grin, I could see that man I saw watching us when the ship left the port at Seattle. I shivered.

Julianne shrugged. "This fellow must be looking for someone else."

"As far as I know, there is just one Julianne Dushan aboard this ship and that's who he asked about," Daniel said.

"How mysterious. Was he good looking?"

"Alice!" Julianne gave her a stern look.

"Not in my opinion," Daniel said.

"It's scary." I scooted closer to my sister. I hadn't told her about the man I saw because it went right out of my head. Now I wondered if I should mention it.

"I'm sure it means nothing." Julianne put an arm around me that was warm and soothing. However, her hand trembled slightly when she reached for a little tin pitcher to pour cream into her coffee.

I looked to Alice for comfort, but her attention was on Dan. With a merry glow, she asked him about playing shuffleboard.

"The deck is still clogged with boxes and baggage. When we hit open sea, I'm afraid it'll be too rough to play then," Dan said with eyes transfixed on her.

"Today is a great time to bob my hair, don't you think, Alice?" She agreed enthusiastically and was willing to leave Dan behind.

In our cabin, with the first cuts, my long braids plopped into my lap. Then Alice's scissors clicked away for more than an hour. As she worked, it was as if she was a different person, serious and all business. At the end of the job, she handed me a bone-framed mirror. Natural waves curled softly above my ears.

"Spiffy. My head is so light." I shook my tresses and ran fingers through it.

Julianne glanced up from a book she was

reading. "It is a very professional haircut, Alice. Look how it enhances my little sister's impish green eyes."

"Real hip, no?" Alice held up another hand mirror to give Tish a view of the back.

"It's perfect! Thanks a million." My snipped braids lay on the floor. "These are going overboard, a burial at sea." I ran out swinging them in the wind. Alice and Julianne followed.

"Look, a whale," Alice screeched. She pointed to a giant hump breaking above the surface. The whale's tail rose up then slapped down on the water with the sound of a rifle shot.

"Here, Mr. Whale. Here's a gift for you." I flung my braided hair into the sea. We lingered out on the deck looking for sea lions, seals and dolphins until a chilly breeze sent us inside.

On the second day out, we were just north of Vancouver Island and into open water. The ship rolled upward, leaning left then downward in a roll to the right. The sky steadily blackened. By afternoon it was raining. The ship was rolling so much that our appetites were gone. Anything eaten came right back up and a rush to the toilet in time was on. By midday we crawled onto our bunks and laid our spinning heads down. I woke up completely refreshed hours later in the darkness of a stormy night. The nausea was gone. My only thought was of sandwiches and pie.

"I'm going to the dining hall," I whispered in Julianne's ear. She responded with a moan. I slipped my raincoat over my nightgown and pulled on boots, then ventured out onto the unsteady deck. The ship continued to roll so I grasped the wet, cold handrail and made my way to the galley.

I found only a few people had come for the usual late-night snack. Lights burned brightly, it was warm inside and smelled of baking bread.

"I see the little lassie got her sea legs," said the waiter with an Irish brogue. He wore a well-splattered white apron over his ample belly. "How be your sister and Miss Allen?"

"They're still sick, but I'm hungry."

"Well then, here you go." He set a steaming bowl of vegetable beef soup on checkered oilcloth. "Now you hold tight to the bowl, this ship is still rolling."

As he returned to the stove behind a long counter, a middle-aged woman walked unsteadily to my table. "May I join you, my dear? It's just not right for a child to be in a place like this alone at this hour. I, too, am unaccustomed to being in a public place unescorted. My husband is down with seasickness."

"Yes, do sit with me." The prim woman reminded me of Sister Agatha, my fifth grade teacher whose favorite subject was etiquette.

The waiter brought more soup and a plate of sandwiches. Mrs. Jonathan Thornton introduced herself as being en route only as far as Prince Rupert, British Columbia. "It will be a blessing to be off this ship so full of questionable-looking men. I fear for you and your two sisters traveling so far with the likes of them." She lowered her voice to a near whisper and glanced about the room.

"My sister is going to Fairbanks to marry a man who struck it rich in a gold mine." She asked me to describe what the wedding would be like. I gave into a storytelling urge and I made up details worthy of a royal wedding. "Guests will include the mayor, governor, and even President Coolidge if he is able to travel from Washington D.C."

By the time I conjured up an elaborate white lace wedding dress, violins and trumpets, a carriage with white horses and a ten-layer cake, Mrs. Thornton's eyelids drooped. At the last bite of her sandwich, she interrupted me. "Let us return to our cabins together, my dear. The decks are wickedly slippery in this storm so I can give you assistance."

I was elated from the drama of the dream wedding and up to any challenge. I immediately became her assistant and let the lady cling tightly to my arm as we stepped out into the darkness. Even though she was bigger than me, she gripped my arm like I was a super-strong girl. I offered to walk her to her cabin, which turned out to be on the opposite side of the ship.

I welcomed the wind pushing against us and rain spraying in our faces. It was cold, but also fresh and clean.

"Oh, we're here at last." Mrs. Thornton grasped the knob on her cabin door. "Thank you, Matisha, for seeing me here safely. Now, do be very careful going on."

"Good night." I bowed politely like any normal hero.

I held onto the guardrail for support, but was in no hurry. There was excitement in the wild, salty air and black splashing waves. As I neared the stern, the moon blinked from behind fleeting clouds and its silver fingers touched quickly over cargo tied there. The black silhouette of a man flashed in an instant flicker of moonlight.

"Is someone there?" I called. Waves slapped, the engine chugged and timbers creaked, but no one answered.

As I got near our cabin, I noticed something that frightened me to the bone. A large wooden crate was unleashed from tie-down straps on the deck. It jogged freely as the ship tilted into a big swell. At the same moment, Julianne came out the cabin door directly in the path of the sliding crate.

CHAPTER 4

Danger on Deck

I heard myself scream as I lunged into my sister, forcing her against the wall. Julianne screamed, too, as we both crashed onto the deck, but out of the path of the crate. It slid within inches of us. It banged, screeched and ripped out a section of the guardrail. The crate plunged into the sea and silver foam splashed toward the moon.

"Hey, is someone down there?" A man's voice called from overhead. "Ross, look! Someone's laying on the deck down there."

My heartbeat pounded so loudly in my ears I wasn't sure where the voices came from. Thudding boots descended from the top deck. In the gold glow of lantern light that bounced toward us, I saw two crewmen. I scrambled to my feet. Julianne sat up with a moan and rubbed her knee. The hood on her cape had fallen away and rain pelted her loose hair.

"Are you ladies hurt?" Strong, wiry arms pulled Julianne to her feet.

"Thanks to my little sister I'm fine." Julianne leaned against the wall. "A runaway crate nearly took both of us overboard."

"It was headed right for Julianne."

"Look at that, Skeeter." Ross stretched over the side to see the crate vanish behind the ship. "I'll be damned if it didn't break loose."

"I saw that happen only once, but that time a real gale was blowing," the bearded Skeeter said.

"You ladies need to get warmed up. Me and Skeeter got hot coffee up in the pilothouse."

"I...I think we could use something warm." Julianne's voice trembled.

"That sounds so good," I said through chattering teeth.

Skeeter helped Julianne limp up the stairs. Ross clasped my hand and we followed. His hand was scratchy, full of calluses, but strong and safe.

Ross pulled open the pilothouse door. The scent of coffee mixed with pipe tobacco and motor grease flowed out into the wind. It was a small room enclosed by windows that looked

29

down on the decks and whitecaps. There were benches along two sides. The tall steering wheel in the center was tied with a rope looped over a post. Coffee perked on a pot-bellied stove. Ross picked up the pot and poured steaming coffee into metal cups.

I added canned milk and three spoons of sugar to mine. "I saw someone, or at least a man's shadow, over by all the cargo."

They stared at me. All mouths opened to speak, but just then, the captain pulled the door open. An instant change came over the two friendly crewmen. They looked like Sister Agatha had caught them with spitballs.

"What's the meaning of this, Ross? You know the rules about women in the pilothouse." A pipe bobbed between his teeth as he talked. I decided Alice would call him handsome in his double-breasted coat, beaked cap, gray-streaked sideburns, and deep, bossy voice.

Julianne pushed wet strands of hair off her face. "These men were helping us, Captain Hale. We were nearly forced into the sea by an unleashed crate."

"What the h.... Skeeter, get on down there and check those ropes. Make damn sure nothing more breaks loose."

"Yes, sir." The crewman was quickly on his

way.

"Ladies, I surely do apologize for this. It is most unusual to have cargo come loose. Be assured I will check into the matter at the first light of morning."

With my eyes on the captain, I sipped my creamy coffee. "Just before it happened, I saw the shadow of a man around the cargo."

The captain's grey eyes softened in a fatherly way. He crossed over to me and he patted the top of my head. "I'm sure one might see many shadows on a stormy night like this."

"Especially young girls and women?" Julianne spit out measured words.

Ross coughed loudly from his position at the wheel. The captain glanced impatiently at him, but made no attempt to appease Julianne.

"Whenever you are done with hot coffee, I will see you both safely to your cabin." Captain Hale tapped his pipe on the stove. Ashes emptied onto the grate and he placed the pipe in his breast pocket.

Julianne took a last gulp. "We're quite ready to leave."

I emptied my mug and raised a hand to wave at Ross. He winked at me.

Captain Hale held the door open for us.

The rain had turned to a sprinkle and the wind to a gentle breeze. Moonlight reflected off the wet surfaces of the deck and made it shine. Captain Hale held Julianne's arm as she limped down the steps to the lower deck.

"May I ask why you ladies were out in the storm so late at night?" the captain asked.

I told him about going to the galley and then Julianne said, "I was half asleep when I thought I heard a knock on our door. I got up and stepped out to see who was there."

"And no one was there?"

"I didn't see anyone until Tish smashed into me."

"Well, Tish, did you hear anything to go with that shadow? Like footsteps perhaps?"

"Wind and waves were all I heard, sir."

"Many things are not what they seem on a stormy night."

"Captain, how then do you explain the loose cargo crate?" Julianne crossed her arms defiantly.

"You both have my apology for that and I assure you I will give it my personal attention. Good evening Miss.... It's Miss Dushan, is it not?"

"Why yes, it is."

He nodded and left us at our cabin door. I was glad he didn't pat the top of my head again like I was five years old.

"Gee whiz, I know what I saw," I whispered when we were inside.

Alice could be heard breathing in a deep sleep. We hung up our wet coats on the hooks next to the door. Like me, Julianne was wearing her nightgown too. We managed to wash up with the water pitcher and basin and used the commode that we would empty in the morning.

"Tish, you saved my life tonight," Julianne whispered and squeezed her arms around me. "I love you."

"I love you too." I kissed her cheek, climbed up to my bunk and nestled my cold feet into the blankets.

I lay awake for a long time replaying the visions of the sliding crate, the shadowy figure, and the stern captain patting me on my head. I decided it's true that coffee keeps people awake. My fingers found the heart stitched on Raggedy's chest. The comforting 'I Love You' embroidered by my mother began to have a soothing effect.

In the morning, there was a thump on the bottom of my bunk.

"Ouch!"

"Was that your head, Julianne? Oh, it must hurt," Alice exclaimed. She fastened her skirt and bent toward Julianne. The calmed sea had returned color to her cheeks.

"It doesn't hurt as much as my knee. I took a fall last night." Sitting up, Julianne rubbed her knee.

"Did you fall out of bed?" Alice's long-lashed eyes were wide.

"No, I heard a knock on our door and got up, but saw no one, so I went out to look for Tish." Julianne dangled the bruised knee for Alice to inspect and filled her in on the details.

"How spooky!"

"But thanks to Tish it's only a bruised knee."

"You're welcome. I like being a heroine," I mumbled without stirring from my pillow. "I'm glad you weren't there too, Alice. I don't think I could have saved all three of us."

"Gosh, that just makes me so, so faint."

"You are probably faint from hunger," Julianne said. "Let's all dress and go get some breakfast. Thank goodness the water is calm this morning."

While we dressed in similar warm skirts and sweaters, Alice asked, "What was that handsome Captain Hale like?"

"He was scary."

"Exactly how I imagine Lew Kelovich will be," Julianne sighed. "He treated us both like children. He was dreadful."

CHAPTER 5

Julianne Fights Back

Next morning we were loading up on pancakes and hot maple syrup when Daniel O'Keefe stopped by our table. I scooted closer to Julianne to give him a spot at the long table we shared with Alice and others.

"That was some fright you two had last night, Miss Dushan. How are you this morning?"

Conversations at the table ceased. Forks stopped midway to mouths hungrier for news than for fried eggs and flapjacks. At least a dozen pairs of eyes turned our way.

I announced, "Julianne's knee is black and blue."

Alice put a soft, cuddling arm around Julianne. "They both could have been killed!"

"Something went overboard," a man at the end of the table bellowed.

"What's the story O'Keefe?" another man asked.

Daniel cleared his throat like he was preparing for a speech. "Someone tampered with the cargo. A crate came loose. The heavy seas last night plunged it clean through the rail."

"Just like I told Captain Hale." I spoke up loudly so men who came from other tables and stood around us could hear.

"How do you know it weren't no accident?" asked a surly voice from a man concealed behind others beyond the end of our table.

"Because the ropes were cut. That's how," Daniel answered.

"That crate was aimed right at my sister!" I pushed aside my syrupy plate. My appetite fluttered away like a butterfly.

"It was rotten luck that Miss Dushan was out at that very minute," Daniel said.

A fist banged down on the table. "What sort of a nut do we have on board?" a man yelled.

"Who's going around shoving things overboard?" someone else grumbled.

Captain Hale's voice boomed from the galley door. "That is something we hope to determine soon." He strode over to our table.

Like a gentleman in the presence of ladies, he pulled off his captain's hat. "It's my guess this is a petty act of vengeance against the Hudson Bay Company who owned the crate. A special watch will be on the cargo from now on. I'd like all of you passengers to help keep an eye out. Report any concerns to me immediately."

Not a word came from anyone. The captain nodded to Julianne and me then turned on his heels, slapped his cap back on, and strode out of the galley.

We left the galley as quickly as we could get away from all the questions. It was good to be out in air that did not smell of frying bacon. A brisk wind whipped my short hair and plastered my skirt tight against my legs.

"So, someone did cut the rope," Julianne mused.

"Captain Hale was proved wrong about me seeing a ghost now that he knows someone was really there."

Alice pulled her sweater tightly around her. "The captain is so forceful. I shouldn't want him angry at me."

"He was really mad about us being in the pilothouse."

Julianne linked arms with Alice. "Imagine such a rule as no women allowed. Such arrogance!"

"But surely, you don't believe your Lucky Lew could be like that."

I grabbed Alice's hand and pointed it at ocean waves. "He could sail this ship better than that old Captain Hale. Lucky Lew can do anything."

Julianne shook her head. "I'll let you be the judge, Alice. Want to read the letter he sent my father to ask my hand in marriage?"

"Oh, splendid!"

"I'll get the letter," I said and took off running for the cabin. I had Julianne's carpetbag open on her bunk when they got to the cabin. I pulled out an envelope addressed to our father. We huddled together on Alice's bed and stared at bold handwriting. It was penned with a quill in blue ink. Julianne read aloud:

"9 April 1925

Dear Jonsey,

I'm deeply saddened to hear the cancer has a hold on you. You know you've always been my partner and friend. As close to me as kin. I've been thinking how I could make it up to you for all those good times. Remember when you pulled my ass out of that ice hole in Lake LeBarge? Well, what I'm offering is to take care of those daughters of yours. By now Julianne is grown to a woman and me, being a single man, am willing to take her in and make her my wife. You know I got plenty of money to insure her and little Matisha a secure future. And, I was thinking, with a young wife, luck just might bring us a son one day and I could name the little fellow Jonah after you. What you say partner? When the end comes, tell your girls to book passage. I'll be waiting and thinking of you with affection.

Your friend to the end.   Lew"

Julianne looked up from the letter. "Do you see the slightest hint that I am to have a say in this matter at all?"

"What he says about your father is so sad." Alice wiped at away a tear on her cheek. "But it does seem he's talking about a horse, not a person. It is hard to imagine you father agreed to this."

"Gee whiz, Julianne. You know it made Papa happy to know Lucky Lew will take care of us."

"That's true." Julianne patted my hand the same way Captain Hale had patted my head. "Because of his poor health, I didn't argue with Papa. However, Mr. Lewiston Kelovich will definitely get initiated into the twentieth century when I get to Fairbanks. I have no intention of marrying him."

Alice's arm flew around Julianne. "When you meet that handsome man, you might fall in love. Then you will have a big, really royal wedding."

"That could happen, Julianne." I thought of the fairytale wedding I told the lady last night.

"Hmmm, could it be you're thinking you might like him after all? Is that the real reason you're going all the way to Alaska?" Alice teased with her eyes twinkling. I really liked Alice knowing she was on my side.

"I want to go to Alaska for one reason only. That is to start a career."

"Doing what?" I quizzed. Buoyed by support from Alice, I had a sense that victory was in sight. Merrily, I probed a pocket in the bag for a deck of cards.

"Maybe I'll teach school, or keep accounts in an office, or work for the newspaper. Don't worry, Tish, we have enough money to keep us going for a while."

"Whatever you decide to do, I know you can do it." Alice enthusiastically shifted her support to Julianne instead of me.

"Let's play Old Maid." I shuffled the cards with vengeance. The empty feeling that we may never be in a real family again swept over me.

The sea stayed calm through the Inside Passage. We could see the mainland on one side and islands scattered on the other. At the charming waterfront town of Sitka, we went ashore long enough to stroll along the boardwalk past historic buildings. In the general store with goods hanging all about, I begged Julianne for a new sweater but she insisted we had to save our money.

By the time the ship entered the Queen Charlotte Sound, my nightmares over the loose crate had faded. Then something happened to jangle my nerves again. A note was slipped under our door.

Alice spotted it first. "Now look at that. Who do you suppose is asking for the pleasure of our company at the farewell dance tomorrow night?"

I scrambled from my bed, and she handed me the scrap of paper that was not addressed to her. "It says, 'To Miss Dushan'. Jeepers, it's in the messiest letters I ever saw."

Julianne took it from my hand and unfolded it. Slowly she translated the scrawled words. "Be smart---get off in Skagway and catch the next boat back!"

"Goodness gracious, that's a threat," Alice gasped.

"We better go tell Captain Hale."

My sister frowned at me and shook her head. "Ask him for protection like a helpless child? I don't think so. Beside, this note appears to be written by someone cowardly. Look at the writing."

"No penmanship award for him," Alice agreed.

"That sure doesn't make it less scary." I put my arms around Julianne.

The rest of the morning we made guesses about who wrote the note and why. Alice guessed it was a past love forlorn over Julianne's betrothal to Lucky Lew. Julianne assured her there was no likelihood of that considering her sheltered life at the girl's school in a convent.

"There were no dates or dancing there, but we did learn to think for ourselves, trust our own judgment." Julianne looked calm, her jaw set stubbornly.

"Golly, in my school, the boys were always the club presidents, school paper editor and team captains," Alice said. "It just seems the natural way of things, though not always fair."

"Not fair at all. But a mean note is not natural, it's scary. I don't want something bad to happen to you, Julianne." I began to snivel like a little kid.

She handed me a handkerchief. "Don't worry. I promise to call the captain and every sailor on board if this rat dares try anything."

"I do big screams too," Alice said as she gave me a hug.

It was a rainy night when the ship stopped at the port of Skagway. Most passengers were asleep. Only a few disembarked. My eyes popped open at every sound outside our door. I stared at the trunk we had barricaded against it. As Julianne had predicted, the *Northwestern* got underway again at dawn and no one had battered down our door.

Bright sunshine in the afternoon lured me to the deck. One look at the spectacular scenery and I raced back to the cabin. "Come see the otters," I called.

Julianne put down her book and Alice stopped filing her fingernails. They followed me to the observation deck to see a pod of sea otters lying on their backs among floating ice chunks.

Someone shouted, "Look, the glacier is calving." Sounding a lot like a cannon firing off somewhere in the mountains, another huge chunk of blue ice broke from a glacier and plunged into the sea. A towering iceberg forced a huge wave to roll before it. The ship jostled in the wave.

Alice and I pressed against the guardrail, but not Julianne. She was missing. I looked all around. "Julianne," I called then spotted her backed up against a wall. I hurried over to her. "There you are. Did you see the iceberg?"

Julianne rubbed her arms, hugging herself.

"Are you cold? What's wrong?"

"Julianne, you look so pale." Alice exclaimed.

"I've had the most irresistible sensation. I could feel someone watching me. Eyes were burning into me. Yet, I saw no one looking my way."

"The man who wrote that awful note." I scanned the deck from bow to stern. But none of the men on deck were staring at us.

"He could be on the deck above." Alice peered overhead.

"Or it could have been my imagination." Julianne lifted her chin.

"I'm glad this trip is almost over," I sighed.

"The best is yet to come. I just know we'll dance every dance tonight." Alice sang, "Charleston, Charleston, let's dance the Charleston..."

Julianne smiled. "We might as well enjoy our last night of overwhelming popularity, for tomorrow we'll be back in a world more evenly divided."

CHAPTER 6

Dance to Peril

For hours we prepared. We took turns in the bathhouse that was shared by other women passengers. Our personal hairdresser, Alice, brushed and curled our hair. She tied a blue ribbon in mine that matched tiny flowers on my cotton dress. Alice told us in detail about a few dances in her life. "I long to hear the music and try to keep up with a man's big feet."

I told my experience at dancing was limited to the Virginia Reel in an all–girl gym class. "This will be my very first real dance."

"And likely your last for a few years," Julianne said. "You're going only because it's the ship's party. I intend for us to leave it early."

"Yes, sister dear." Not only was I excited, but felt lucky to get to go and actually dance.

At eight o'clock sharp, the three of us

walked into a transformed dining hall. It was cleared of tables and rang with lively music. The musician was a man who played a harmonica and an accordion at the same time. Just steps inside the door, both Julianne and Alice whirled away in the grip of men who stomped to the beat of "Camp Town Races".

"Come on, Matisha. Want to give it a try?" asked Daniel O'Keefe.

"Can you teach me?" He laughed hard and tugged on my hand like it was a ship's rope. I hung on and skipped to the middle of the floor. In time with the music, he pumped my arm up and down. I felt like we were priming a pump so water would spill from a well.

Every time the tune changed so did my partner. I was kind of getting the hang of it. Dodging stomping boots kept my feet dancing. There were few ladies, about twenty, and more than a hundred men. My stamina was severely tested as I followed instructions from one clumsy hoofer after another. Only when the musician took short breaks did I get to sit down for cookies and orange punch. Time slipped by. At nearly midnight, Julianne insisted we leave. I did not argue. Alice said she would stay a little longer.

"Dances are fun but my feet hurt," I said with a yawn. "I danced at least a hundred times."

"My feet may never be the same either." Julianne wiped her brow with a lace handkerchief. "The cool outdoor air feels refreshing."

"And smells a whole lot better than sweaty men." We both laughed.

Even though it was midnight, the northern summer sky was still aglow. Outside the galley, a few couples held hands and swooned over the brilliant red sunset afterglow reflected on dark waves. As we walked away, the rest of the ship was deserted and immersed in shadows.

"That's odd," Julianne said. "Look how dark all the cabin windows are. The gaslights must be out. I won't get to read in bed."

"Wait here, I'll get you a lantern." I hurried back to the galley and removed an unlit lantern from a hook on the wall.

I swear I was gone less than thirty seconds. When I headed back, the setting sun was in my eyes but I could see something odd in the shadows. It was Julianne and she was not alone.

A man had Julianne in a grip around her waist and his hand was over her mouth. He had her head yanked back and I heard him snarl, "I'm warning you, bitch, if you know what's good for your pretty hide, you won't be getting off in Seward. Go back where you came from or else..."

I let loose a horrendous scream and charged. I landed a running kick to his shin and whacked him with the lantern.

"Ouch! Damn!" He cussed as he slammed Julianne to the deck. His boots pounded as he fled toward the stern.

"Julianne, are you hurt?" I tugged on her arm.

She scrambled to her feet. "I'm okay, super girl. Let's get inside before that scream of yours brings a crowd."

In the cabin, I bolted the door with shaky hands. Julianne slumped onto her bunk, rubbed her hip, then her shoulder.

"Oh, Julianne, he did hurt you." I put my arms around her. "I didn't see him very well, but I could tell he was really, really big."

"Actually, he wasn't much taller than me, but strong. Tish, you were so brave."

"He was just awful! He told you to go back to Seattle."

"That's what he told me, but it'll take more than a bum like him to convince me." She frowned, more angry than scared.

"I'll go get Captain Hale as soon as Alice gets here so you won't be left alone."

"No, you won't. I'm perfectly safe in here." Julianne struck a match and lit the wick on the lamp. "Since we didn't see who my attacker was, the captain can't help."

"Jeepers, he could have killed you. Please don't die and leave me all alone." Invisible icy fingers gripped my heart like when Mama died and again at Papa's funeral. I buried my head in my sister's lap.

"I'm fine. Everything will be just fine when we're off this ship and board a train to Fairbanks. You'll see." She caressed my back.

"It'll be fine only if you do marry Lucky Lew. Please say you will, Julianne." My plea was as desperate as I felt.

"We'll see," she said very softly.

A ray of hope crept over me. Maybe our family would get whole again after all.

We got into nightgowns and for almost an hour, I lay in Julianne's comforting arms. While waiting for Alice, we reminisced about good times spent with Papa.

As soon as we heard the sound of a cooing voice, I unbolted the door then climbed into my bunk. We waited and waited. Mumbling on the other side of the door went on and on. Her sugary voice said, "Good night" again and again. When she finally came in, her face was flushed and glowing.

"I'm so glad you're still up. I'm bursting to tell you... I think I may be falling in love." She bent to untie her shoes.

"Well, Alice, you and Dan do make a super looking couple," I said.

"Yes, Dan is nice too. Gosh, he's really nice, now that you mention it. But so is Chuck. Oh dear, it's so sad. After tomorrow, I may never see either of them again." Alice looked at me, then at Julianne.

She waited for an answer to her dilemma. We didn't offer any. Alice frowned. "Tish, why are you awake so late? Oh, Julianne, your cheek is scratched. What happened?"

Calmly bolting the door, Julianne began to tell of the attack.

"How awful. Do you know who he is?" Alice nearly collapsed onto her bed.

"We didn't see his face," I answered.

"But, with his chin at about my ear level, that would make him barely a half head taller than me." Julianne held a hand above her head. She wrinkled her nose and added, "His acrid

back to cabin 22.

"Did you hear that?" I shouted.

"We heard the train whistle," Alice said. She hurriedly yanked on straps fastened on her bag and pulled them through buckles.

"Tish, come get your carpetbag." Julianne took our coats from the wall hooks and carefully folded them into her bag.

"Gee whiz, I think the train will leave us if we don't hurry." I tugged on our trunk with all my strength toward the open door.

Daniel O'Keefe appeared. "I'll get that trunk for you ladies. No worry, the train won't leave until ten and it never leaves on schedule anyway."

"Thank you, Daniel," Julianne said. She tossed her carpetbag on the cart that he wheeled up to our door. I heaved mine on too.

"You ladies will have time for breakfast ashore." His gaze settled on Alice.

"I hope you can join us, Dan." With a dazzling smile, Alice handed him her bag.

"I can't be getting off for a couple more hours." He shrugged then hoisted our trunk onto the cart.

"Perhaps we'll meet again someday."

Alice's sleepy eyes added softness to her pretty face.

"Sure hope so," he said with a wink and pushed the cart toward other waiting luggage bound for the railway platform.

"Goodbye, Dan," I called. He retreated to the stern and waved back at us before he was out of sight. We joined a string of passengers on the gangplank. I turned back to see the big ship. As it emptied out, it began to look deserted.

"Oh, is the land moving?" My feet were wobbly after so long at sea.

"I feel it too," Julianne said with a chuckle.

"Whoa, me too." Alice put her arms out for balance.

I skipped unsteadily ahead on a boardwalk that fronted a line of shops. A sign that read 'Seward's Folly Cafe' stopped me. "Isn't that what people used to call Alaska?"

Julianne nodded. "When William Seward negotiated the purchase of Alaska from Russia in 1867, most of America thought it a real folly."

"Let's see if Seward's Folly has good food," Alice said.

I pulled the café door open. The smell of frying fish filled the air. Indecipherable conversations filled the room. I rushed ahead to the only unoccupied table and slid into a chair woven out of twisted birch branches. Alice sat beside me. Julianne sat across the polished birch wood table. Sunlight streamed through red checkered curtains.

Alice picked up a hand-printed menu that lay on the table. Her eyes widened. "Yikes, look at these prices."

"Maybe we should settle for oatmeal," Julianne said.

"I'm not very hungry after last night," I said. "I had the most awful dream."

"Me too," Alice chimed.

Julianne said, "I spent the whole night fighting off a demon." We each described our spooky dreams until the waiter brought us steaming bowls of oatmeal mush and a pitcher of milk.

Alice scooped sugar into her bowl. "What if that bad man gets onboard the train?"

"What if he's a..... killer?" Oatmeal caught in my throat.

Julianne toyed with her spoon, turning it slowly in a stream of sunlight. "If he were a killer, he would have tossed me overboard when he had the chance. His intent was to scare me into not going to Fairbanks. I wish I knew why."

"It doesn't make sense." My worry must have been obvious because Julianne reached across the table to hold my hand.

"Wow!" Alice exclaimed. She stared over Julianne's shoulder, her face glowing. "Take a gander at who just came in."

"He looks like a barnstormer to me." With a new focus, I absently spooned more sugar onto my mush.

"Such a handsome one, don't you think, Julianne?" Alice whispered.

"I'm not turning around to gawk. What's so impressive about him?"

Alice continued to whisper. "At least six feet, blond wavy hair, mustache, nice shoulders and the rest is all muscle."

"Around his neck is a long white scarf like flyers wear in the movies," I added.

"Sounds a bit flamboyant. So what's he doing?"

"Just standing in the doorway," I said.

"And looking around with heavenly blue

eyes, and, and... Oh goodness," Alice gasped. "He's coming this way."

Julianne shrugged. "Then, I'll judge for myself when he walks by."

"He's looking right at us," I whispered.

"Good morning, ladies. I'm Leif Bjorgam of Rainbow Flight Service. I assume one of you is Miss Julianne Dushan just off the *Northwestern*?" He sky blue eyes looked directly at Alice then Julianne.

We looked at each other with shared apprehension. I shook my head at Julianne, warning her not to answer.

"Well?" His stare settled on Julianne.

"Why do you want to know?" Julianne asked.

"When Lew Kelovich found out I was flying down here from Fairbanks, he charged me with an urgent message for Miss Dushan."

"How exciting." Alice's doubt was forgotten.

My head was full of the nasty man who attacked Julianne. What if this was another one with the same idea? I opened my mouth to bombard him with questions, but Julianne interrupted my plan.

"I understand Fairbanks is over 400 miles away? No flying machine can go that far." Julianne stared at him accusingly.

"Apparently your aeronautical knowledge is behind the times. By chance, could you be Miss Dushan?" He stared back at her.

Julianne hesitated, their eyes locked on each other. Finally she nodded.

"I'm her sister, Tish." If he turned out to be a villain, at least this time we knew his name and what he looked like.

"I'm their friend, Alice Allen." Alice offered her hand and smiled sweetly. "It must be a very important message. You came so far and by such extraordinary means."

He wore a handsome smile as he shook hands with each of us. "Pleased to meet you Miss Allen, Miss Dushan, Tish." He pulled out a chair and sat next to Julianne.

"You flew to Seward for your Rainbow Company?" I asked, liking the name and wondering if it could be a good omen.

"I flew down here to get crates off-loaded from a barge that was in port a couple days ago. I had to get the parts of a new aircraft aboard the railroad. It's an airplane that will make a big difference in passenger and cargo service."

"What is the message you bring Mr. Bjorgam?" Julianne said with suspicion in her voice.

He tensed, cleared his throat, and diverted his eyes to a saltshaker. "Mr. Kelovich has been in an accident."

"Oh mercy, an accident." Alice's hands flew over her heart.

"What happened?" I asked. My feet and hands went cold.

"The brakes on his Bearcat gave out on the summit road. It rolled down a ravine." He demonstrated by spinning the saltshaker over the tabletop, but caught it as it fell towards the floor.

My spoon slipped from cold fingers. "Was Lucky Lew hurt?"

He nodded.

"How badly?" Julianne asked.

"He's had multiple fractures, which would heal in time if it weren't for pneumonia. I'm sorry to say, Dr. Noble is afraid he won't last long." With a fingernail, Leif scraped at grains of salt encrusted on the saltshaker lid.

"But he is a strong man." My voice trembled.

Julianne looked down at the table and spoke sharply. "So you've come to urge me to return to Seattle. To tell me the bridegroom is no longer interested in marriage. Is that it?"

Leif blinked, taken aback by the bite in her words. "Heck no. He wants me to fly you to Fairbanks so you two can get hitched before this day is over."

Alice sighed, "How romantic."

"Really?" I cried mildly, but inside I was screaming, *Hooray*!

"If he is so sick, why would he be anxious to marry?" Julianne looked at him as if he was not quite real.

"Something about his will, in the event that he does not survive. He's really determined. As you know, Lew Kelovich is used to getting his way about things."

"The truth is I have very little knowledge of that. However, I see no reason to not believe what you are telling us."

Leif looked intently into Julianne's green eyes as if he was trying to figure out what she could possibly mean by that.

"You intend to fly Julianne away today?" Alice asked breathlessly.

"We're going in an airplane?" I jumped off

my chair.

"That's the plan if she agrees." Leif's open hand pointed at Julianne.

"Julianne loves all kinds of adventure so this is the right kind for her," Alice said.

"Not necessarily," retorted Julianne.

"Sure it is," I said. "And besides, it'll be safer than the train."

Leif tilted his head, looking more puzzled, but then he smiled broadly. "There never was a safer plane than the Standard. I'll have you there by supper time."

"There is no such thing as a safe flying machine," Julianne said.

Alice reached across the table to squeeze Julianne's hand. "Being on the train for two whole days means anything could happen. It scares me to think of it."

Leif leaned forward. "Miss Allen, it is true that this is the first year the Alaska Railroad has run all the way to Fairbanks, but it has a clean accident record."

"Oh, it's not that we're afraid the train will crash or anything, you see...." Alice stopped when I jabbed her with my elbow.

"All right," Julianne said abruptly. "We will

fly to Fairbanks with you."

Leif glanced from one of us to the other like he wasn't sure what we were all about. He shrugged. "It's settled then. We'll leave as soon as you're ready. I've been waiting around for a day and a half."

"I presume you were amply paid for the wait, Mr. Bjorgam," Julianne snapped.

The pilot studied the cool eyes that frowned at him. With a faint grin, he said, "Friends call me Leif." I was beginning to like Leif Bjorgam, the handsome, dashing pilot of flying machines.

The blast of the train whistle startled everyone in the cafe.

"Time to get on board," announced the man behind the counter. The cafe began to empty with chair legs scrapping on the wood floor, loud cheerful voices and silver dollars plunked down by the cash register. Leif insisted on paying for our meal, saying Lucky Lew had given him an advance for expenses. I wished I had ordered sourdough hotcakes.

When we set out for the depot, I noticed my land legs were steady on the boardwalk. The walkway turned into a dirt path. There was excitement in the morning sunshine that sparkled off deep blue water and lit up tall mountains encircling the town. Many squawking gulls drifted over the harbor. A couple of eagles in the treetops watched us all the way to the railroad platform. Through the crowd, I spotted the luggage cart tended by a uniformed porter. I hurried to the cart with Leif.

"Tish, show me which ones belong to you two."

"This one, this one and this one." I slapped my hand on the trunk and both carpetbags.

Julianne came up behind me. "Surely the airplane can't carry all of that."

"The Standard is a work horse, but the trunk is better off on the train." Leif retrieved only the carpetbags.

A burly, bearded porter offered us advice. "It don't pay to get in too big a hurry. If you want a guarantee of getting to Fairbanks, you young ladies will climb up those steps and leave that flying to daredevils." The porter gave Leif a villainous glare before he trudged off with the loaded cart.

Leif shrugged and strode off toward the station window, saying he wanted to make sure his crates with the new airplane were loaded. Passengers and townspeople milled around. Steam belched in a cloud from the locomotive. Wood smoke heavily scented the air.

"The train is so shiny and looks as new as they say it is," Alice said.

With a hush, Julianne said, "Somewhere among all these people, I should be able to spot that man." We huddled together and searched faces.

"Maybe that one." I pointed at a whiskered man in a battered wide-brimmed hat. He hastily stepped into a passenger car and disappeared.

"Watch out for that one, Alice." Julianne said.

"Don't worry about me. It's you two up in the air that's truly scary."

"All aboard," the conductor shouted. Alice lunged into my arms for an energetic hug. "I'll keep my fingers crossed for you both and for Mr. Kelovich."

"My fingers are crossed for him too." I blinked away a tear and looked up at the blue sky. "Gosh, soon we'll be flying over the train."

Alice pressed me hard to her bosom. "The thought makes my heart race."

"I can hear mine beating too." I pulled away and touched my throat. My heartbeats were rapid.

"Mine too," Julianne admitted. "But flying

is the only way to get there quickly."

"My sister knows how to be a nurse." I thought of how she tended to Papa day and night.

As Leif walked back to us, Alice enveloped Julianne in a hug. "Leif, you take good care of my friends."

"They're in good hands. A Rainbow plane has never crashed." Leif handed Alice's bag to her. She stepped onto the train steps.

"I hope, hope, hope to see you on Wednesday," Alice called as she boarded the train. Tears glistened on her long lashes.

"We'll be at the train station to meet you," I called.

The locomotive engine hissed in a series of steaming chugs, as it pulled away from Seward.

CHAPTER 8

Dragonfly Airplane

Townspeople who came to see the train off, switched their attention to us. Leif led the way with all the confidence of a celebrity. His white scarf fluttered down the back of his tapered leather jacket. Trooping after us were fishermen, mothers with babies, and kids younger and older than me. A couple of muscular men volunteered to carry our luggage. About half a hundred people followed us down a dirt road that sloped to the beach.

When we stepped on the pebble beach at low tide, Julianne stumbled over rocks. I grabbed onto her arm. Unlike my lace-up shoes, Julianne had worn stylish high-heels for riding on the train.

"Leif, how far to the airfield?" I asked.

"You're walking on it."

"An ordinary beach is the airfield!"

Julianne exclaimed.

"I've never seen a beach with no sand, just rocks, but look, Julianne, there's a monster sitting on it." I pointed at what looked like a giant man–made dragonfly resting near a rock jetty.

"There's the flying machine," a boy shouted. His brown face glowed with the wonder of the universe.

"Ah. Ooh," the crowd sang like a choir.

"Oh dear." Julianne squeezed my hand.

"Amazing." That was all I could say. My skin tingled all over.

"Are you really going for a ride in it?" asked a small blond boy.

"Of course they are, Dummy," snapped his teenage sister. She and her two companions huddled together and eyed our dashing pilot. They whispered and giggled as our parade came alongside the winged machine.

I was fascinated to see wires tied the four wings to the body. It had two open holes, one for the pilot and one for a passenger.

I noticed all color drained from Julianne's face. She turned to Leif. "Do you really intend to take off from here?"

"This strip is a heck of a lot better than most," Leif answered. His all-business eyes scanned us critically. "You'll need coats. It'll be a chilly ride."

With jittery hands, we rummaged through our carpetbags, pulled out coats, and stood there watching our pilot. He picked up our bags to load them into the plane, and said, "You two hop into the front seat."

Leif got busy removing the guy wires that tied the wings to the ground. A couple of men held onto the wing tips to keep the plane steady. They asked technical questions. He told them the two gas tanks were full and held sixty-five gallons.

In a loud voice that all his fans could hear, Leif explained, "With ideal weather like today, this 150-horse engine could power us to Fairbanks in four hours if we went straight through, but we'll stop in Anchorage for more fuel."

Hearing Leif say that sparked me with a brilliant idea. Climbing up onto the flying machine gave me a thrill as if boarding a roller coaster. I reached for my sister's trembling hand. "If we make it as far as Anchorage and we hate flying, we could catch the train when it gets there."

"If we make it?" Julianne moaned. It was

not a modest moment for her in a short skirt. She had to step high for the footholds exposing more leg than she cared to show. Embarrassment turned her face from pale to crimson. Her whole body slightly trembled as we shared the single passenger seat. I liked the closeness of being crammed in. We were definitely in this together.

As Leif released the last of the tie-down lines, the teenage girls stepped as close as they dared. "Is your passenger a movie star?" one asked. "She looks like Miss Clara Bow."

"She's even prettier," another giggler said.

Leif chuckled. "I'm guessing she could be a movie star if she chose."

He stepped up to the cab holding leather helmets and goggles. "Not too glamorous for a would-be movie star, but you'll be glad to have these."

Julianne snatched them out of his hand, but did not express her obvious annoyance with a comment.

I pulled the leather cap over my ears and fitted the goggles to my eyes. I felt like I was wearing a superman disguise as I peered down at the crowd. "These people are so friendly. You must fly here a lot."

"Just once. This is the first time anyone has landed in Seward."

"The first time?" Julianne's eyes went wide.

With a grin, Leif set a sheepskin rug at our feet and stepped back down to the rocky shore. Julianne breathlessly whispered to me, "Can you see what he's doing now?"

"He's just reading a map." I could see him on my side. "It says 'Alaska Railroad' on it."

"Oh great! A map for a railroad, not a map for the sky."

"A map is a map." She nodded as if she wanted to believe me with all her heart. "Lucky Lew really wants us to get there so you can help get him well."

"Oh, Sweet Matisha, I have such regrets for exposing you to such danger. You should be on the train with Alice. It's crazy to have us fly in this weird contraption." She kissed my cheek.

"I'm your sister so I need to be with you. Besides, flying will keep us from worrying even longer about Lucky Lew." I spotted an eagle swoop toward the rolling sea and pointed it out to Julianne, hoping she clearly sees our wondrous new world.

Leif spread the map out on a wing and took his time studying it. Then he folded it, stuffed it inside his jacket and walked to the nose of the plane.

He pulled on the propeller and the plane vibrated a moment. He pulled again. By the third hard tug, the engine growled to life.

"Hooray," shouted the crowd over the deafening roar.

"Hooray," I shouted too.

Everyone backed away, leaving the beach clear. Leif hopped effortlessly up into the cockpit behind us, fastened the straps of his cap and adjusted his goggles.

Julianne pulled her cap and goggles on. We sat waiting for the engine to warm. Daniel O'Keefe and Skeeter from the *Northwestern* came running up the beach. I waved. They shouted something but all I could hear was the engine becoming increasingly loud.

Slowly we began to move. The Standard bounced along the beach, going faster and faster. Its tail rose. Its body bounced some more, then rose above the pebbles for an uncertain minute. The whole flying machine bounced one last time before rising into a breeze.

Leif kept the nose level for a few

seconds. I turned to watch him tug gently on the stick that was beside his knees. We began to climb as the engine thrust forward at top speed. The plane banked to the left, then straightened out. It climbed over the ocean then turned back toward land. The engine roar softened and seemed like steady music.

Julianne held onto me with her eyes squeezed shut. When Leif abruptly tipped the plane, she squealed. He made the wings wag at the waving crowd below. I decided it was better than any roller coaster in the world. We were over the people, over the docks and ships. Flying felt awesome.

The crowd grew tiny then disappeared as the beach faded away. There were only mountains. Giant slopes were ahead of us and on both sides. The singing of the guy wires, rush of the wind, and the engine's steady hum were the sounds of the world on high. Leif smiled when I looked back at him. I gave him thumbs-up and the biggest smile I had in me.

Julianne opened one eye, than another. With all our options gone, I could feel my sister relax a little and hoped that would allow her to absorb this fantastic experience too. She pulled the woolly sheepskin blanket over our legs as wind chilled us.

Leif pointed to the ground ahead of us and way below us. The train was winding along on a tiny black line of track at the edge of an inlet. It seemed impossible to imagine a tiny Alice could be on that miniature train. I wondered if she was looking up and seeing us.

The scenery was beyond anything that I could have imagined. Mountains crowned with glaciers rippled endlessly until they dropped away into the sea. There were green valleys and too many lakes to count. For well over an hour, there was no sign that people might live somewhere down there in the vastness. Nor was there an airstrip or farm field where an airplane in trouble might set down. There was nowhere to land until, beyond a brilliant multi-colored rainbow, there appeared the houses and streets of Anchorage.

We circled over the town, getting lower with each circle. People came out of buildings with faces turned up to us. They hurried to gather on the edge of the airfield. In a wide circle, we dipped toward seawater and then I held my breath as the ground rushed up. Julianne buried her face in her gloves. The plane touched down with a thud and bounced along on gravel. When Leif finally shut down the engine, people clapped and shouted.

I waved, feeling like part of a dazzling miracle. I scooted out of the plane and onto the field. Pushing my goggles to the top of my cap, I faced the crowd and was hit with a barrage of questions. Where had we been? How long had the flight taken? Where were we headed? Would we take letters to friends and a package to a brother in Fairbanks?

Julianne tugged me away with a whisper about finding a powder room. We left Leif to work at getting the plane refueled. It was a short walk to a small cafe on the edge of the field. When the door opened, the fresh breeze blowing sweetly from the inlet was replaced by the smells of frying hamburger.

Beyond a long lunch counter was the cafe's washroom. I was as relieved as Julianne to find the facility unoccupied. After I pulled the chain on the commode, I was startled at my image in the mirror. The leather cap, with goggles on top, had my hair smashed down. I pulled the goggles back over my eyes. I looked a lot like a frog, but liked what I saw.

"Wasn't that just the greatest adventure in the world, Julianne?" I took the cap and goggles off again and ran fingers through my hair.

"So far we're alive, but we've got 300 miles to go." It didn't sound much like a complaint or a worry. I spotted a hint of excitement in my sister's eyes as she fluffed out her hair. With hands were under the faucet, I playfully flicked drops of water at her. She pulled a towel from the rack and snapped it at me before going out the door.

I trotted after her to a small table. We ordered the first thing the waiter suggested. Steaming plates of stew were set before us at the same time Leif came in and strode over. He pulled a chair out with its legs screeching on the linoleum.

"We ordered the moose stew for you. The first moose I ever ate." I passed him a basket of warm bread.

"That was to save cooking time," Julianne added.

"Stew's fine with me." He grinned. His goggles were perched on top of his helmet.

"Oh Leif, I just love flying," I said. "It's so nifty to be over trees and rivers and everything."

"Glad to hear it, Tish. How about your big sister?" We both looked at Julianne.

"I'm glad we can get to Fairbanks today. I'm very anxious to see for myself that Lew Kelovich is, hopefully, recovering."

"Don't count too much on that. I know whatever happens to him will make a big difference in your life."

"A really big difference," I said and felt a chill of uncertainty.

We ate in silence for a few minutes then

Julianne glanced across the table at Leif. "How long have you been flying around in Alaska, Leif?"

"All together I have nearly 500 hours in." Pride glinted in his eyes.

"Hours?" I asked.

"Aviation hours. I came up from Idaho a year ago last May, accompanying crates that brought the Standard. We assembled her right in Fairbanks."

"But why did you chose Alaska?" Julianne asked.

"I thought only gold miners came here," I said.

"I wanted to fly, but not as a barnstormer or for Mexican revolutionaries. Rainbow Flight Service needed a pilot and I took their offer."

"Wow, you had scary choices." I decided Leif was truly fascinating.

"Yes, and with so much distance between places here, perhaps you made the most risky choice." Julianne sounded as if she was needling him.

"Risky in more ways than distance." We waited for him to explain and he squirmed as if he regretted saying that. "I'm buying into the business.... slowly."

"Aren't airplanes just for joy hops?" I thought of advertisements in the Seattle newspaper.

"That certainly seems more like a game than a stable sort of business." Julianne sounded like she was ready to argue.

Leif put down his fork and looked really serious. "In this country, aviation is far more than a game. It is transportation and it is the future. We can fly mail to places in one day, where dogsleds in the winter and riverboats in the summer take weeks."

"You mean you actually fly in the winter?" Julianne leaned more into the table.

I poured honey in circles to mark a biscuit like an airplane circling above an airfield. "How can you keep from freezing?"

"We'll be able to this year with the Fokker. That's the plane on those two flatcars on the train." There was no stopping him now. He continued, saying the plane was a monoplane with enclosed cockpit and 4-passenger cab. The more he explained about hinged rudder pedals and the aerodynamic of the new plane compared to the biplane that we were flying, the more enthusiastic he became. I didn't understand much, but couldn't help notice how Julianne listened as if she was totally captivated.

As soon as our stew was eaten, we left the café and strode onto the airfield. On this pleasant summer day we were an attraction. A swelling crowd had come to witness our take off. Like in Seward, Leif played to the crowd with his showy, white scarf trailing over his handsome leather jacket.

"Look at that man strutting around like he's on a stage," Julianne said when we were settling into our seat.

"He's just answering questions." I gave her a frown for being less than fair with Leif.

"So you're a fan of his, aren't you?" Her arms went around me with affection. The engine fired to a roar so I answered with a nod. She smiled as we bumped across the field and gradually rose into the air. This time her eyes were wide open, but we both tensed when the water in the inlet rippled just feet beneath us. We gained height above land and the town quickly faded away.

Minutes out of Anchorage we approached the glaciers and snowy slopes of towering Mt. McKinley. Many miles later Fairbanks appeared, and that big mountain was still in view behind us.

CHAPTER 9

The Groom

I looked down on rivers and knew this was where Papa panned for gold. The Chena flowed into the broad Tanana River. Lakes and dark spruce trees dotted expanses of green muskeg. Shimmering birch and aspen trees covered the hills and a few cabins appeared along dirt trails. The plane skimmed over willows along the riverbank, a cluster of buildings, two paddle-wheel riverboats, wagons, automobiles, dogs and people. Circling, we gradually lowered, and everything grew from miniature to real life size.

Leif set the Standard down on a landing field and taxied up to a barn-shaped hangar. The engine sputtered to a stop, leaving me with pangs of regret. The flight ended too soon for two reasons. Not only did I want to be back in the air because of the fantastic thrill, but arriving, at last, filled my senses with dreadful uncertainty.

Leif's strong arms lifted me to the ground. His blue eyes twinkled with as much reassurance as a ray of sunshine.

"You did it, Leif. We're here in one piece." I took in a deep breath and twirled about to take in the empty expanse of the airfield.

"Where are all your fans?" Julianne asked as Leif held a hand up to her.

"The population here is used to aircraft coming and going." He waved a hand toward a man trotting out of the hangar. "Howdy, Jess."

"Welcome to Weeks Field." The short, stocky man in grease-spotted hat and overalls had a gravelly voice and wore a broad grin. He wiped his mechanic hands on a rag, gregariously patted Leif on the back and shook hands with Julianne, then me. "I put in a call up to the mansion when you were circling."

Leif introduced him as Jess Yonkers and expounded on his mechanical wizardry, his wife, and his four children. But my attention had frozen on the word *mansion*. Leif and Jess retrieved our carpetbags then they began to putter about the airplane.

Julianne and I pulled off our flight caps that felt hot in the warm, sunny day. My bobbed hair was sticky and flat. Julianne's hair bounced in neat waves to her shoulders. We handed the caps and goggles to Leif.

"Leif, how is it you know Lew Kelovich?" Julianne asked. The color in her cheeks heightened.

"Everyone knows Lucky Lew in this town. Probably everyone in the whole Territory."

"What sort of man does he seem like to you?"

He pulled off his leather cap. In disarray, his moist, blond hair glistened in the bright sunshine. His face, tilted sidewise, was full of questions. "Don't you know what he's like?"

"Well, I..."

"Julianne hasn't seen him for a long time," I chimed in.

We all turned toward the rattle and thump of a Ford car driving onto the runway.

"Looks like that young lawyer, Mills, is coming to pick you up." Jess Yonkers said.

In a cloud of dust, the car came to a halt. A young man dressed in a business suit hurled himself from it, leaving the engine run.

"Miss Dushan? I'm Steven Mills, attorney at law for Mr. Lewiston Kelovich. Your fiancée desires your immediate presence at his bedside." He spit out the words a mile-a-minute. "I'm afraid his health is in a serious state."

"Of course, we'll go at once," Julianne responded. She clasped my hand and we stood there dumbly while Leif and Steven Mills loaded the luggage into the compartment on the rear of the car.

Then the lawyer extended a handshake to Leif. "Thanks for bringing Miss Dushan here safely, Bjorgam. Terrific job."

"The flight was exciting," I said, causing the lawyer to look at me for the first time. It was kind of a startled look. His head bobbed up and down at me.

"Anytime." Leif said with a grin and pulled open the car door. Playfully, he grabbed hold of me and lifted me into the seat.

When Julianne took Leif's hand, there was no playfulness about him. He almost whispered, "To answer your question, I have to say one thing. What Lucky Lew is not, is the sort of man for you. Not to my thinking."

Steven Mills revved the car engine. Leif put our bags in the open seat then shut the door. The car bolted ahead. I squeezed close to Julianne's ear. "What did Leif mean?"

"I can't guess," Julianne murmured.

It was a short distance to the first cluster of houses. Steven Mills raised his voice over the Ford's motor.

"I'm sorry your arrival is not met with happier news." His boyish good looks made me decide he was sincere.

"Surely, Mr. Mills, this is nonsense about an immediate marriage." Julianne tensely leaned toward him.

Steven frowned and shook his head. "Judge James Wickersham, an old friend and a famous congressman, has consented to act as justice of the peace. He should be there when we arrive."

"But why?" Julianne sounded out of breath.

"He is determined his estate not go to his former wife. Marriage to you would reinforce his will," Steven Mills said.

"He was married?" I exclaimed.

"Perhaps your father didn't know he was once married to Stella Malone. It lasted about ten months. They divorced a full five years ago." Steven Mills looked embarrassed to deliver distressing news. His ears burned bright pink and he stared straight ahead down the road.

Julianne anxiously searched in her purse. I could tell that her distress was not over an old marriage but the impending one. The air in the car was so tense I hardly noticed all the storefronts we passed. I could almost hear my sister ponder how she would get gracefully out of the nuptials. My heart raced as fast as hers. It's true I had wanted her to marry Lucky Lew, but now everything seemed topsy-turvy.

"Look, the railroad depot," I shouted much louder than needed. We rolled onto a narrow bridge over the Chena River. "Alice will be there tomorrow night. Right?"

"Yes, it'll be so good to see her." Julianne pulled her hat from the purse.

"I wish she was here right now." I watched Julianne fumble with her flapper hat. She pushed the long strands of her hair into it, leaving her to appear neat and composed.

The Ford turned into a driveway that circled through a regal row of tall birch trees. It stopped before a replica of a southern plantation-style house complete with white columns and an expanse of mowed lawn. The house faced away from the riverbank.

Before we could walk up the steps to the front door, it opened. An elderly man looked at us with sad red-rimmed eyes. He wore overhauls and a plaid shirt with sleeves rolled up, revealing the loss of his left hand.

"Slim Goodwin, may I present Miss Julianne Dushan? And, oh yes, this is her sister," Steven Mills said.

"My name is Matisha Dushan!" I said in my most annoyed tone.

My indignation was lost on the old man who merely nodded his head of unruly white hair. He walked away without even saying 'how do you do' like anyone would expect.

"This is a stressful time," Steven said in an apologetic way. "Although he's not overly friendly in the best of circumstances," He led us into a spacious foyer with a polished hardwood floor. "If you'll wait here, I'll announce your arrival." He disappeared through double doors at the end of the foyer.

Julianne crossed over to the ornate mirror above a table that held an immense vase of blue delphiniums. Her hands trembled as she smoothed her short skirt and pushed a stray strand of hair under her flapper cap.

"Wait," I whispered. "Goggle marks are still on your cheeks."

She pinched her cheeks until the creases were replaced with a rosy flush. When the attorney's face abruptly appeared behind us in the mirror, we both jumped. My pulse banged in my throat.

"Sorry to startle you." Distress gave his voice a high pitch. "He's asking for you."

"How is he?" Julianne asked.

"I don't know how he hangs on."

We followed Mr. Mills passed a living room where heavy drapes were drawn against the afternoon sun. We stopped at open double doors to the study. The first thing I saw was a portrait above a massive desk. It was of a robust man with piercing dark eyes. I ventured a few steps into the room while Julianne and Steven Mills walked forward. Two men were next to a sofa where a pale likeness of the portrait lay propped on stark white pillows.

Lucky Lew's black and gray-peppered hair was damp with perspiration. His eyes were splotched with red, deeply encircled with darkened flesh. A plaster cast covered his left leg. He was freshly shaven and wore a crisp white shirt with a black bowtie.

"Jonsey's daughter. Good." His words were in short gasps. He motioned to a white-haired, distinguished-looking man in a dark suit.

"This is Judge Wickersham," Steven said quietly. The judge nodded to Julianne and reached calmly into his briefcase. He produced a leather-bound book.

Lew Kelovich held out an unsteady hand to Julianne. Kneeling beside him, she clasped the moist, chilled fingers in both her hands. He immediately slipped a gold-nugget ring onto her finger.

Julianne gasped. Kneeling there, she did not look too steady. I quickly knelt beside her in case she needed me to hold her up.

"Julianne Dushan, do you take this man to be your lawfully wedded husband?" the judge asked in a deep, solemn voice.

As if the judge had slapped her face, Julianne stared with eyes wide and mouth open.

I slipped an arm around her waist and whispered, "Don't upset the poor man."

Julianne blinked at the ring, the sick man, then at Judge Wickersham. The judge frowned at her. Her lips formed a silent 'no' but her head nodded 'yes' as if weighing the consequences.

I pressed against her ear. "Go ahead, it is best."

"I...I...do," Julianne sputtered.

The judge let out a breath. "And

Lewiston, do you take this woman to be your lawfully wedded wife?"

"Yes," the sick man wheezed.

In a satisfied baritone, the judge proclaimed, "By the authority vested in me by the Territory of Alaska and the United States of America, I now pronounce you man and wife."

CHAPTER 10

A Day Without Night

Lew Kelovich's limp fingers tugged on Julianne's hand. "I was wrong. Jonsey saved my life. He was my partner. It's right for his daughters to have it all. God forgive..." A convulsive cough seized him.

The doctor, with a stethoscope dangling from his neck, nudged Julianne aside. I jumped out of his way. The doctor poured whiskey in a shot glass and held it to the sick man's lips.

Tears sprang to Julianne's eyes. "Whiskey? Has he had any food?"

"Ain't touched a bite in three days," Slim said. I spun around to see him in a dim corner of the room seated in a wooden rocker. The bookshelves next to him were filled with leather-bound books and dotted with carved pieces of ivory, soapstone and jade. Slim's whole body drooped helplessly.

The patient's coughing eased and Julianne leaned close to him. "Mr. Kelovich, you've got to get well."

"You got to!" I echoed. My stomach quivered with the same frantic spasms I felt when Papa was so sick.

"Do you think you could eat a little soup?" Julianne said.

He nodded weakly. His eyelids looked heavy, wanting sleep.

Julianne turned to Slim. "Mr. Goodwin, could you?"

"Come on, the kitchen's this way." A glimmer of hope strengthened Slim's voice. He rose stiffly from the rocker and walked out the door.

"I'll be there in a minute," Julianne called. She removed Lew's necktie and handed it to me. She loosened his collar in an effort to ease labored breathing. It was like watching her tenderly nurse Papa all over again.

The sick groom closed his tired eyes and appeared to breathe more easily. With a hanky from her pocket, Julianne wiped moisture from his forehead. A certain peace came over his face. His chest heaved up and down, up and down. Then it stopped.

The bowtie slipped from my fingers and fell onto his chest. Julianne stared at the motionless chest. She turned to the doctor.

"Stand aside, please," the solemn doctor commanded.

Julianne put her arms around me. We moved toward the breeze coming from the large window. It was open to colorful flowerbeds. I twisted around to watch the doctor press his stethoscope on Lucky Lew's chest.

"How is he, Dr. Noble?" Steven Mills asked.

The doctor wagged his head. "He's gone."

My eyes were drawn to the portrait above the fireplace. It held me as if I was in a trance. It seemed alive, strong, and invincible. The doctor pulled a sheet over the motionless body.

"Tish, come. Let's go find the kitchen. We need to tell Mr. Goodwin." I took my sister's outstretched hand. It trembled in tandem with my own.

We passed through an expansive dining room to swinging doors that led into the kitchen. The kitchen was well equipped with a water pump on the sink, an icebox built into the wall, a sturdy table and a silver-trimmed wood-burning cook stove. A row of windows looked down upon the Chena River. The long counter was littered with bowls of prepared food and loaves of fresh bread wrapped in cloth towels.

"Neighbors brought in all this stuff," Slim said when we entered. "This ptarmigan soup is still warm from lunch. A ptarmigan is like a wild chicken, Lucky's favorite." He lifted the lid of a pot on the stove. Steam released the rich aroma of vegetables and meat.

Julianne placed a hand on the old man's shoulder. "Mr. Goodwin, the doctor says that Lew has passed away."

My eyes filled with tears for the old man who had lost his friend.

Slim replaced the lid on the pot and slumped into a chair at the table. He buried his face in his one hand. I stood next to him and reached out to touch his shoulder.

Julianne moved the big soup pot to a cooler spot on the stove. She left the room saying she needed to talk with Steven Mills. I slipped into a chair next to the old man. My whole body was weak with his sorrow and my own deep disappointment. My dream of a new family had died.

Julianne had no more than walked out of

the kitchen when the arm with no hand came down on the table with a horrific bang. Startled, I jumped out of my chair.

"Someone's to blame. Lucky's been murdered." It was as if Slim was spitting words made of dirt. My watery blur of a broken old man cleared instantly. I no longer looked at a sad man. This man was angry.

"It was an accident. Didn't the car turn over, Mr. Goodwin?" I wiped the wet off my cheeks with the back of my hand.

Slim ran a fingernail along a little scratch etched in the top of the kitchen table. Muscles in his wrinkled face were tight. His voice became quiet as he mumbled. "Didn't I check that car out regular? Nothing was wrong with them brakes and no one drove better than Lucky. There's been foul play. He knew it and I know it."

I sat back down across the table at a safe distance and tried to think of some way to cheer him up. I reached across and put my hand on his arm. "Papa said Lucky Lew was the bravest man he ever knew."

Slim looked at me as if I had just dropped in from the moon, actually noticing me for the first time. "He was." His voice strengthened to a rasp. "Lucky could go down white rapids in a rowboat without batting an eye."

"Papa said he once ran off a whole pack of wolves and saved the life of a baby moose."

"Well, that's one I never heard." A sidewise grin pulled on a corner of his thin lips. "That pappy of yours was a fine man."

Julianne came through the swinging door. "Mr. Goodwin, you knew our father?" Compulsively, she began to tidy up the kitchen.

Slim nodded. "Jonsey was a real friend to me and as close to Lucky as a man could be."

"I suppose that's why Papa wanted Lucky Lew to marry Julianne, then," I sighed with my heart aching.

A tin cup clamored to the floor. It had fallen from Julianne's hand as she turned away from the sink. She yanked the large gold nugget ring from her finger and set it on the table. "I have no right, nor any want of this."

Slim put his hand over hers. "You got more right to it than you know. Please keep it. It was Lucky's dying wish." He pleaded in a slow-talking way.

With an urge to set things right, I picked up the cup and carried it to the sink. As weird as it was, it seemed too soon to completely give up my dream. "At least think about it for a while, Julianne."

Julianne's eyes glistened with uncertainty. She picked up the ring and dropped it into in her skirt pocket.

We heard doors slam somewhere in the house. Julianne explained, "According to Steven Mills, that will be men from the funeral home. The judge and doctor will leave with the body."

We were all out of words. Slim pumped water at the sink and filled a kettle. He put it on a hot burner. Julianne handed me bowls to set on the table and I found silverware in a drawer. The house was quiet when we settled at the table for bread and bowls of the succulent soup. The three of us ate without joy.

After dinner, we talked about Lucky Lew. Slim repeated his story that Lew had been the victim of an evil plot. He insisted the car wreck had not been an accident. Since there was no diverting him, Julianne promised we would check out the accident site in the morning.

Slim exhaled with relief. "I got the know-how on fixing automobiles but I leave the driving to younger folk with two good hands."

"Julianne took the automobile driving course at the convent and she passed." I smoothed honey on a slice of bread.

"Do you trust a woman driver?" Julianne

asked. I knew it was true that most men did not.

"Jonsey was one of a darn few men Lew trusted all the way. Now he's put his trust in Jonsey's daughter. Reckon I'll do the same, lest the day comes it don't prove smart."

"That is fair enough." Julianne tossed a towel to me and poured hot water from the kettle into a dishpan.

The June midnight sun rolled along on the edge of the horizon, barely setting. Our conversation slowed down as the house filled with long shadows. A clock in the foyer chimed ten times when Slim bid us good night. Julianne and I climbed the stairs and found our bedroom was at the first door in the long hallway. We had our own bathroom and I started running water in the tub. It was good to see the lawyer had carried our carpetbags to the room.

We could finally put this astonishing day to rest. Today we had stepped from a ship onto Alaska soil, climbed into a flying machine, soared into marriage then widowhood. All this happened in the space of one day. It was a day that had no night.

Was it real? I wondered, as I fell into exhausted sleep beside my sister and Raggedy Ann.

CHAPTER 11

The Bearcat Crash

I awoke to mysterious sounds in the strange, expansive house. A rhythmic tick came from a glass-enclosed pendulum clock. It sat on the fireplace mantel in our bedroom, with its hands pointing on Roman numerals VII and VI, telling my sleepy brain it was half-past seven. Footsteps thumped somewhere downstairs and a door clicked shut. I guessed Slim Goodwin was up moving about.

Auburn hair spilled across the pillow next to me. "I'm so thankful to have the sunlit night over," Julianne moaned.

"You turned and turned." I said with a yawn. "Did you have dreams?"

"I did. I was airborne and a pilot's neck scarf blew across my face so I couldn't see where I was going."

"Was the pilot Leif Bjorgam?" I laughed

and rolled out of bed. "In my dream I chased the train, running and running, trying to catch it."

Julianne was content to lie back on pillows. She watched me dig through my carpetbag and put my few things in a laundry pile and spacious drawer. Abruptly, she stood up, stretched and began to straighten the bed. "With daylight all night long, it's a wonder we slept at all."

I pulled on a cord that dangled from the window shade. Sunshine streamed through lace curtains onto the Persian carpet. Bright rays glistened on the wedding ring as it lay on top of the dresser. I touched a finger on its gold nugget that was as big as an Indian head nickel. A ghostly shiver swept over me.

Julianne was out of bed in a flash. She snatched up the ring, slipped it into a drawer and slammed it shut. "That's something I cannot face today. Not yet." She shuddered. "Let's get dressed. Slim Goodwin is sure to be waiting."

"Okay. I can hardly wait to see the wrecked car." Without our trunk, I had to wear my same sailor dress. I partly covered it with an old sweater the color of dead grass. Julianne tied on a brimmed hat, but had no walking boots in her bag so she slipped on her pumps.

We found Slim in the kitchen heating milk in a saucepan. With hot cups of cocoa, we lingered over slightly stale cinnamon rolls made by a neighbor. Slim passed a big jar of honey. "Bees make this from the fireweed flower. It comes from the Bentley homestead." His words were spoken in a slow, thoughtful way. "We'll ride by there today."

I tasted a spoon of honey. "Really yummy, Mr. Goodwin."

"Like everyone in this territory, I want both you ladies to call me Slim."

Until that moment, I never knew an old man whom I would dare not call mister.

Julianne smiled. "That will be our pleasure. Now, Slim, tell us how long it'll take to drive to Cleary Summit."

"Don't worry, we'll be back by early afternoon. Long before that train gets here with your trunk."

"And get Alice here." I thought how much there was to tell her. Alice would surely be a bright spot in the dismal days to come. Slim struck me as really thoughtful to know that the train could not get to Fairbanks fast enough for me.

As soon as I dried the last dish, I slammed out the screen door and ran to the

Model-A Ford parked in the driveway. The seats shone with polish, as well as all the parts inside and the winged ornament on the hood. Impatiently, I watched Slim and Julianne walk slowly down the back steps. They stopped twice, looked at each other and kept talking. It took all my willpower not to urge them to hurry. I wanted so much to get on our way to solving the mystery, if there really was a murder mystery.

Julianne got behind the steering wheel. Slim went to the front of the car and turned the crank. The car shook, then howled to a start and he hustled into the front seat.

The road to Cleary Summit was dusty and full of ruts. We bounced along beside birch trees and willows. A breeze whipped the leaves, making them flicker green and silver.

We didn't try to talk much over the noisy engine and bumpy road. But I shouted when I spotted moose. Standing in a pond, there were three of them, a big gangly one and two cute baby moose. Julianne ignored my plea to stop the car. I snapped my head around as we passed by and the moose disappeared behind trees.

After almost an hour, the Ford started to climb up a steep mountain. We were near the top of the summit when Slim shouted, "Stop here."

Julianne parked on the side of the road and pulled hard on the hand brake. I jumped out and peered over treetops covering the downside of the hill.

Slim's suntanned hand gestured out the open window. "I was told the spot is along here somewhere."

"The trees are so thick. That's all I can see," I said. The scents of spruce and dust enveloped us.

"Let's walk up the road and keep looking," Julianne suggested with her shoes making wobbly steps on gravel. Further up the hill we could see nothing on the downside except forest.

"Well," Slim said with labored breaths. "Maybe we should drive up the hill and search some more."

I ran ahead to the Ford. Julianne ambled slowly with Slim so I ran farther down the hill. As I looked over the edge where the ravine had a steeper incline, a flash in the sun caught my eye.

"I see it," I hollered. A ways below, the white hood of the Bearcat glimmered through trees and brush. Slim and Julianne walked briskly down to me.

"Follow me." Slim led the way though

spruce trees and brush. Julianne slipped along in her ladylike shoes. Her high-heels and my boots dug into the spongy, moss-covered forest floor. It was moist and had a fresh, green smell. The wrecked Bearcat lay exposed on smashed brush.

"It's demolished." I was stunned to see a totally mangled roof.

"How did Lew survive this wreckage at all?" Julianne shook her head.

"Lucky Lew drove it down from the Pedro Creek Mine." Slim took off his hat and pointed it at the mountaintop. "That's the mine he started with the one and only Jonsey, your Pa."

Staring up the high hill, I felt touched by the sound of true warmth Slim gave to mentioning Papa. With his sleeve, Slim wiped perspiration from his furrowed brow. "Lucky was trapped for most of the day, all cut up and broken in a cold rain. Only a stroke of luck kept him from dying right here."

"Who found him?" Julianne asked.

"Bud and Riley took a notion to go to town and came down from the mine. They spotted skid marks that ran off the road and found Lucky smashed against the steering wheel, like a wounded grey wolf caught in a hunters trap."

The vision sent my eyes searching the deep forest for wild animals. Seeing none I swallowed the lump in my throat and scooted under the car. Under a maze of bent steel, it smelled of grease and gasoline. My fingers touched an odd cable that dangled freely. "Holy smokes! What is this, Slim?"

Slim squatted to peer under the car that was wedged at a tilt against a birch tree. Up to squinting eyes, Slim held a few broken threads that dangled from the cable."Son of a...." He muttered cuss words under his breath. "Just what I thought! That <u>was</u> the brake. You can't stop no motor car without a brake cable. This one was cut on purpose."

Julianne bent down to see under the car. "Who would do such a thing?"

"And why?" I gasped.

"It beats the devil out of me." Slim wagged his head back and forth. "But I figure Lucky Lew had his share of enemies."

I crawled out from under the car. "Maybe someone from the mine cut the cable?"

"Ain't been no trouble up there lately." Slim sat down on the moss-covered, fallen tree.

Julianne clung to a spruce branch to keep her balance on the steep slope. "Perhaps the damaged cable just happened to give out coming down that steep grade."

"It weren't no secret he went up to the mine a couple times a week, and always on Monday."

"And, you say it happened on a Monday." I began to feel a little like Sherlock Holmes. "Let's call the police."

"Yes. We better bring this to the attention of the authorities." Julianne dug in her heels and started the climb up to the Ford.

I wanted to run up the steep grade in front of her but slowed to keep pace with Slim. Part of the way up the hill Slim said with a wheeze, "It won't do no good to tell Constable Dole."

I asked him to explain but he just wagged his head and panted for breath. Nor did he say more when we were out of the ravine and back on the road.

Thinking like a Sherlock, it became clear to me that we had more than one mystery. I pressed forward from the back seat, close to Slim's ear. In my loudest voice over the motor and rattles, I told him every detail about the threats against Julianne on board the *Northwestern*.

Julianne didn't interrupt. She was

absorbed in coasting, then braking down the twisted mountain road. The Ford stopped at the curb on Cushman Street under a sign marked City Hall.

"It was really scary, Slim," I said to conclude my story.

"That is the damndest, most confounding thing." Slim gave my arm a pat.

"I wonder if there could be a connection between the threats aimed at me and that cut cable," Julianne said.

Slim frowned. "If it's about a secret Lucky Lew had, it died with him. He didn't talk much about personal type stuff."

"Somehow, we've got to find the answers." Julianne pounded her gloved hand on the steering wheel.

"Let's start with the constable." I hopped out of the car.

"Good luck," Slim called as he leaned back in the car seat, preparing to doze off.

Julianne and I marched into the City Hall building. Inside we stopped at the reception desk. It was vacant. I ventured toward an adjacent door and pressed my nose on a frosted window. "Someone's in here."

I pushed the door open.

We caught a big man in the middle of a yawn. He sat behind a desk laden with a newspaper and magazines. His protruding stomach tugged at buttons on a blue, starched shirt. Julianne's heels clicked and my boots clomped on the wood floor. His eyelids snapped wide open and color rose in his pudgy face.

"What can I do for you today, Mrs. Kelovich?" He gave a little cough and straightened in his padded, leather chair.

"You know who I am?" Julianne was startled to hear herself called that, and so was I.

"It is my job to know what goes on in this town." He spoke with a southern drawl. "By tomorrow, when the paper is out, the whole town will know about your nuptials."

"Then, Constable Dole, you will be interested to know Slim Goodwin has discovered foul play is involved in the death of Lewiston Kelovich. The brake cable on his Bearcat was purposely cut causing brake failure on that mountain road."

"Now, now, young lady, I know imagination can run real wild when someone is grieving over a loved one."

"It's not imagination..." My mouth shut fast as his booming voice butted in.

"The fact is that this here is a peaceful town where the deceased was beloved by everyone. After you're here for awhile you'll see that."

"If you will go with us to the crash site, you will see exactly what the truth is," Julianne said.

Springs in his big chair squeaked as he rocked backward. His round face filled with a smirk as he gazed up at the ceiling. A portrait of President Woodrow Wilson above his desk showed more interest in our story than the sleepy-eyed constable. The stubborn set of his whiskery jaw made it clear that nothing short of an earthquake would budge him.

"You're not going to investigate?" I gave him a shocked glare.

Constable Dole leaned forward. The chair squeaked again. "I'm telling you nobody in this town had cause to harm Lew Kelovich. Next time you come in here telling me there's been a killing, bring me a reason for it too. That's when I'll start doing some investigating."

Julianne met his defiant stare and returned it. "All right, we will."

"We'll be back," I added in a sassy way and followed Julianne out of the office. Our heels pounded on the board floor. I shoved the front door so hard it slammed.

I hopped into the car while Julianne turned the crank. "That old constable didn't believe us," I complained to Slim.

The engine throbbed to life and Julianne rushed into the driver's seat. She squeezed the wheel and stared straight ahead.

Slim put his hand on her arm. In a slow, calm voice, he said, "With a little tad of luck, I'm believing we can root out the killer."

"Yes we will, Slim." Julianne covered his hand with hers. "We'll get proof and Constable Dole will have to listen."

I slapped the back of the seat with both fists. "So much proof that lazy, fat man will have to budge!"

"Matisha, watch your tongue." Julianne's tone was a scolding for name calling.

Slim grinned, turned to me and winked.

Julianne released the brake, and the car lurched like a frog before she managed the clutch and gas pedal. The Model A bolted to top speed, spewing dry river silt into a cloud that drifted toward the open window of City Hall. Onlookers across the street, beside Anderson's Drug Store, shook their heads. The men looked like they shared one opinion, that machines and females ought not mix.

I waved at them, busting proud of my sister. I figured people in this town would see a challenge to old fashioned ideas from now on.

CHAPTER 12

The Train Arrives

In the afternoon a neighbor, Tilly Waters, arrived with a plate of fresh baked cookies. Slim introduced her as the cook who came in three days a week. Tilly bubbled over greeting us. Her rhythmic speech and accent announced her Swedish origins. She squeezed Julianne's hands and took me into her chubby arms. Her gray-streaked hair smelled of vanilla.

"By golly, you sweet things have come all this way and don't deserve the ordeal of it all," she said. "Now sit right down for a cup of tea."

Slim backed out of the kitchen saying he was going to take a nap.

"Thank you for the lovely cookies, Tilly," Julianne said as we sat down at the table.

"Plain sugar cookies were a favorite of Mr. Kelovich." Tilly's eyes filled with tears. She poured boiling water over tea leaves in a ceramic teapot decorated with tiny blue flowers. I turned away as she dabbed her eyes with a hanky.

"I'll get the tea strainer. Tea and cookies, like a real tea party." I peered into one drawer after another until I found a wire strainer.

Tilly held it over delicate cups and poured brewed tea. "Now, both of you young ladies must be exhausted. After tea it will be best if you be off for a nap."

"I'm not sleepy," I said and reached for another buttery cookie.

Julianne set down her tea cup. "Really, Tilly, we prefer to be busy. Don't send us away to be idle and mope about until it's time to meet the train."

Jumping to her feet, Tilly first put an arm around Julianne then she gave me a hug. "You are not only sweet, but wise. Come on, let us all work like beavers in a stream. Work is good medicine for breaking hearts."

This rosy-cheeked woman with her mothering way was a real comfort, but we didn't go about our tasks much like beavers. We talked and puttered in the kitchen.

"This big house needs a really good cleaning, I'm afraid," Julianne said with a broom in her hand. "It's a little overwhelming to think of how much needs to get done before the funeral."

"Now, don't you try doing it all by yourself. Lew Kelovich hired Emmy Petrokov and her daughters for laundry and cleaning. She's a good Athabascan woman. If you want, I'll go by her house and ask her to come see you."

"Thank you, Tilly. That would be a big help," Julianne replied.

"How old are the daughters?" I asked, thinking how good it would be to have friends.

Tilly added a handful of flour to a mound of dough in a big bowl. "I believe Helen turned thirteen and Sissy is almost eleven. They are bright, lovely girls and clever with beadwork."

She talked nonstop as she turned the bread dough onto the counter. I helped knead it by jabbing it with my fists. She told us all she knew about the housekeeper Emmy, who was married to a Russian fur trader.

When the bread dough was covered with a towel and left to rise, Tilly handed me an onion to chop. Before long, I blinked back onion juice tears. Tilly browned the onions in a skillet sizzling with bacon and added a slab of beef. The scent made me guess, "I'll bet pot roast was also a favorite with Lucky Lew."

"It was indeed." Tilly smiled and began a long story about Lucky Lew. She called him a true friend, praising him for coming to her aid when her husband fell ill and missed a season of work. I decided we could scratch Tilly Waters from a list of murder suspects.

When the kitchen filled with a yeasty fragrance, Tilly took off her apron. Before she left the house she said, "Take the bread pans out of the oven in another thirty minutes from now."

I followed her out the back door. "Tilly, what if we have to race to the train depot?"

"There'll be no need to head for the depot until you hear the first whistle blow. That's when the train will be at the foot of University Hill." Tilly gave me another hug and rode off on her bicycle.

I lingered in the warm sunshine to listen for train whistles. On the path near the river, mosquitoes buzzed around my head. When I finally heard a faint whistle in the distance, I ran back to the house and called for Julianne.

"I'm up here." I found her upstairs brushing her hair.

"I heard the train whistle. Let's go."

Julianne ran the hairbrush through my straight, chin length bob. "We'll go as soon as you wipe flour off your shirt and your cheek."

"The bread! I almost forgot the bread." I hastily rubbed down with a towel and ran to the kitchen. I pulled Tilly's bread from the oven. The crust was a little too dark, but it smelled wonderful.

We hurried out to the Ford and found Slim ready to turn the crank. Julianne slipped into the driver's seat. I hopped in and scratched an itchy mosquito bite on my arm. When the motor came to life, I waved goodbye to Slim.

We chugged out of the long driveway and onto the main road. Time seemed to drag as we followed one other automobile and three horse-drawn wagons. The sound of the train was still distant when Julianne turned into the parking lot at the train station.

"Look, there's Leif." I jumped out of car the second the motor rattled off. "Hello, Leif."

He waved from the platform where a crowd waited for the train.

I ran up to him. In my excitement, I blurted, "Guess what, Julianne got married and then became a widow. All that since we saw you yesterday."

Leif blinked like cold water splashed in his face. "So, Lew Kelovich passed away?" He looked over my head at Julianne. "I'm sorry to hear that."

"It's really sad," I said.

Julianne only nodded and turned away from the intense blue eyes that were fixed on her. I felt a need to rescue her so changed the subject really fast. "How come so many people are here to meet the train, Leif?"

His arm wrapped around my shoulders like we were old pals. "Most people are here to see the flatcar unloaded with the new airplane crates." His chest puffed out with a dose of pride. "The *Daily News-Miner* story has the whole town excited."

Julianne brightened to have this to talk about. "I imagine the construction of it will be a complicated project."

Leif beamed. "We'll start tomorrow to assemble the parts. If all goes well, I'll be flying it in a few weeks."

"Will you have it ready by the 4th of July?" I asked.

"We had better. Joy rides are about sold out." Leif's gaze was not on the approaching locomotive. He looked down at Julianne, studying her. "But I'll save a spot for you, Tish. I mean, that is, if you both want to do that sort of thing after what's happened."

The train whistle blew and glistening metal loomed in sight down the track. The engine came puffing toward us. "You bet," I cried over the din of screeching brakes and belching steam.

The train came to a complete stop and people began to descend from a passenger car. Julianne gave Leif a nod before hustling away with me. We saw Alice was the first passenger to step off. Before Julianne and I caught up to her, she flung herself into the arms of a man who I presumed was her father, and a mother and little brother joined in squeezing her.

"Alice, Alice," I called.

"You're here!" Alice exclaimed. "You really did fly all the way here."

"You flew on an airplane?" asked the boy.

"It's a miracle." Alice gave us hugs and a strong whiff of her lavender perfume. She introduced us to her father, mother and brother Patrick.

Mr. Allen, who wore a suit and tie, politely removed his brimmed hat. "We've heard," he said solemnly and bowed his head. "We do extend our sympathies."

"Daddy, what do you mean...sympathy?"

"Mr. Kelovich has passed away," Alice's

mother said gently.

"Oh, Julianne and Tish, I'm so sorry." Alice reached out to Julianne's hands.

A lump tightened in my throat but I managed to say, "We have tons to tell you, Alice."

"I'm so glad you're here at last, Alice." Julianne held both of her hands.

"Do come home with us, my dears," said Mrs. Allen. "Please join us for dinner and tell your story." The laugh lines that creased the corners of her eyes caused me like her instantly. Her plump figure was in a black skirt and white cotton blouse with thin, hard-to-iron pleats down the front and a big bow at the collar.

I flashed a hopeful look at Julianne. "Let's do that."

"Thank you, Mrs. Allen. We'd love to celebrate the return of your daughter with you, but we need to take care of our trunk first."

Mr. Allen offered to have it delivered to the Kelovich mansion.

"I'll show you which one is our trunk," I said and walked with him to a flatbed wagon loaded with boxes and luggage. Our trunk was easy to spot. Mr. Allen called to a porter to make the arrangement.

I ran back and to waited with the others for him. Alice greeted me with another hug and continued to chatter about her train trip.

When Mr. Allen returned, he gave his daughter a squeeze. "I hope you got all the educating you need, sweetheart, because your family missed you."

"I know you think poorly of beauty school, Daddy, but I am very glad to be here." Alice rested her head on his shoulder for a moment. He picked up her bag.

As we all walked to the parking lot, Patrick gave his father's sleeve a tug. "Can I ride in the Ford car?" Please. Can I?"

"You mean, May I," corrected his mother.

"Yes, son, you can show them how to get to our house," Mr. Allen replied after Julianne gave him a positive nod.

Patrick made guttural engine sounds while he ran ahead and hopped on the car's running board. He had rosy cheeks, skinny legs in short pants and the same long lashes as his sister. Hopping inside, he rubbed the leather upholstery with his palms. "I'll bet Madame Urina used to sit right here when she rode with Lucky Lew."

I settled onto the front seat. "Who's Madame Urina?"

"She's a witch that was married to Lucky Lew."

"Really?" I was willing to pretend with him. "Do you know where this witch is now?"

Brown, curly hair got in my face as Patrick pressed into me with his nose almost up to the windshield and pointed across the river. "Right down there on that side of the river. She's a fortune teller."

Julianne slid into the driver's seat. "What are you two talking about?"

"Witches and fortune tellers," I said. Patrick settled his feet on the floor in the back seat.

Mr. Allen turned the crank on the Ford. We vibrated on the first turn. He waved and returned to a horse-drawn, surrey carriage where Alice and her mother huddled in conversation.

Patrick reached up for a hand grip. "Riding in a Tin Lizzie is super. Dad is getting one next summer. He'll order it right after Christmas."

"Automobiles are okay. But airplanes are a lot better," I said.

"Did you really fly in an airplane to get here?"

"Oh, yes. We were the first people to ever fly an airplane from the port of Seward."

"Gee, was it scary?" Patrick's eyes popped as wide open as possible.

"It was super exciting."

"That's what I want for my birthday. A ride in an airplane."

"When is your birthday?" Julianne asked. We rode over the bridge and down Cushman Street. All the while, Patrick bounced behind me, never sitting.

"I'll be nine next Thursday. It's the new airplane that I want to fly in and go really high in the sky."

"Well, first the new airplane will have to be put together." Before I could elaborate on my superior knowledge, Julianne interrupted.

"Are we getting close, Patrick?"

"Turn, then pull on the brake." Patrick pointed, with his arm brushing across my face. "We're here."

We parked in front of a log house with a vegetable garden flourishing in front. Patrick ran to the front door and held it open. He led us through a narrow storm entry into an open area with the kitchen, dining table, and living space. Family pictures lined the walls and flowered pillows were scattered on a sofa and chairs. The walls were logs mostly covered with burlap.

"Alice's bedroom is almost done and Mom's pantry too," Patrick explained. He pointed toward bedroom doors and at a ladder leading to a sleeping loft. The house was filled with the succulent smell of baking chicken, and I thought of the food Tilly had prepared today for us and Slim.

I spotted a telephone sitting on a small end table. "Should we call Slim?"

Julianne quickly picked up the telephone, turned the crank and asked the operator for the Kelovich home. The call to Slim was brief and she hung up just as Alice burst through the front door.

"On the way here, I told my parents everything that happened on the ship."

Mrs. Allen followed her with a frown on her kind face. "Please go help your father with the horse," she told Patrick.

He ran out the door and Mrs. Allen turned to Julianne. "I don't like the sound of your misadventures on board that ship, Julianne. It was very strange indeed."

"It was mysterious, but..."

Alice interrupted, "Oh, do tell us everything that's happened since you got here. I can't wait to hear."

I kept quiet and let Julianne explain the odd wedding ceremony and Lucky Lew's sudden death. When Mr. Allen and Patrick came in, Alice sobbed out the tale all over again. During dinner, we talked about the good times on the steamship like my haircut, seeing whales and the dance. Discreetly, we did not mention Alice's romantic interludes with handsome sailors. I told about flying over mountains, rivers and rainbows. That started Patrick begging for a joy ride for his birthday.

After dinner and the dishes were done, Alice, Julianne and I went for an evening stroll. The summer sun was high in the evening sky and the air warm.

"Alaska is a strange land," Alice said. "It looks like noon but it's almost bedtime."

"In June, it never gets dark so it's hard to sleep at night," I said. We walked on a boardwalk beside picket fences.

Alice sighed. "Sleep has to be impossible in the light and thinking about Mr. Kelovich dying on his wedding night."

"What's worse is that his death was no

accident."

"Tish, what can you possibly mean by that?" Alice's surprised eyes grew wide. Julianne explained how we found the cut cable on the Bearcat.

"Oh dear! You should catch that train tomorrow and no later. It's sure to be dangerous here for you." Alice stopped, too stunned to walk.

"I don't want us to leave, Julianne." The possibility of leaving made my stomach do a flip.

"Nor do I, Tish. What we want is to solve the murder." Julianne gave me a squeeze. She picked a blossom from a row of violet delphiniums growing against a fence and handed it to me. I tucked it behind my ear. We walked on at a slow pace.

"Whatever can you do?" Alice asked.

"The funeral is Saturday. After that, there's the settling of the estate," Julianne said.

"Does all this mean you are now wealthy ladies?"

"So much has happened, and much of it does not make sense. I surely don't feel we have a right to Lew Kelovich's money."

"It's a good guess he wanted you to have

it." Alice threw her arms in the air. "Why else would he get you on a flying machine in Seward while a Justice of the Peace stood by?"

"Julianne and I know Lucky Lew was Papa's really good friend."

"I feel there's more to it than that. But, one thing is for sure," Julianne said. "I've got to find out who cut that cable."

"<u>We</u> have to find out." I insisted.

"Okay, Tish, it will be we who find out."

I grabbed her hand and gave it a shake. "There must be someone who did not want you to marry Lucky Lew."

Alice leaned in close so even squirrels could not overhear. "I'll bet he had a jealous mistress."

"He had an ex-wife."

Julianne added, "The lawyer did mention one Stella Malone."

Patrick jumped out from behind a bush. "She is a real witch."

"You little eavesdropper." Alice held up a scolding finger.

"Patrick, you said Madame Urina is a witch." I edged next to him.

"The witch has two names."

"Now, Patrick, run along to the house this minute," Alice ordered.

He stuck his tongue out at his sister. "It's true. Everyone knows she's a real witch and a fortune teller too."

"Run along, little brother. Scat!"

Patrick shrugged and trotted toward home.

"Maybe the witch is also a killer," I said.

"It is dollars to doughnuts the killer, whoever it is, will be at the funeral," Alice said.

"The funeral is a good place to start," I said.

Julianne put an arm around me. "We're going to get to the bottom of all this. We owe that to Lewiston Kelovich."

"You will help us, won't you, Alice?" I asked.

"Of course. I'll begin by asking questions of everyone I meet. Getting information should be a snap when I start having the ladies in for hair styles."

As we strolled back toward the Allen home, Alice told us about her train trip in breathless detail. I could almost feel the sway, smell wood smoke and hear wheels grinding on the steel tracks. "When the train stopped for the night at the Curry Station, there was this friendly and very good looking guy."

I laughed. "That doesn't shock me, Alice."

"How about that handsome pilot?" Alice's eyes sparkled. "Did he make a pass at you, Julianne?"

"No, he did not. I assure you his mind is exclusively on flying."

"Flying is the best adventure ever. When I grow up, I'm going to be a pilot." It surprised me to hear my voice say that. Deep down, I felt electricity tingle in my toes and light up my heart. In that moment, I knew for certain that someday I would fly an airplane.

CHAPTER 13

Secret Letters

It was midnight when we drove back onto Cushman Street. The wheels churned up dust clouds and the motor sounded louder than ever as we passed through the sleeping town. The twilight sky was tinted in shades of purple and pink. Gusts of wind rattled the long arms of leafy birch branches stretched over the driveway. The big house loomed darkly. Eerie shadows spread over the white columns and across the long porch in the low, lingering, June sun.

"The house is big and spooky." I gulped and gripped the safety stirrup on the car door. "It looks full of secrets. Like maybe it's haunted."

The massive front door flung open. Filtered light from inside made a silhouette of a tall figure with flowing, silver hair and beard. A man raised a bare arm that ended in a stump instead of a hand.

I gasped.

"Hello, Slim," Julianne called.

I had seen a monster, but it was only Slim. My cheeks were red with embarrassment as I brushed past him, mumbled goodnight and bounded up the stairs. Besides feeling foolish, my jittery nerves left me exhausted. I lost no time getting into my nightgown.

When I awoke late the next morning, I was struck with a sense of wonder. I looked about me and said out loud, "So this is Lucky Lew's house." That repeated over and over in my head while I poured water from the pitcher into the basin and washed up. As I pulled on my boots and blue denim dress, the same thought rang in my ears. This house was all about Lucky Lew.

I went in search of Julianne. She was beside me in the night but I didn't feel her get up. I could hear a piano playing, yet I hadn't noticed a piano in the house.

From the landing above the stairs I gawked about feeling like a visitor to a cathedral in a foreign land. Descending one stair at a time I saw things I had been blind to the day before. There was a painting of snowy Mt. McKinley full of green trees and stalks of bright pink wildflowers. The banister was sturdy and polished to a shine. My footsteps clicked on the slate floor in the foyer. The tall grandfather clock ticked with each swing of a shimmering pendulum. It was nearly ten o'clock. In the sitting room, the piano rested on a red and blue carpet. A wake-up fragrance of coffee steamed from a cup atop the piano.

Julianne gently pecked out a familiar song. The words came to me so I sang out the words. "*Look for the silver lining whenever a cloud appears in the sky.*"

With dreamy eyes Julianne glanced at me and stopped playing. "This piano is in tune and it's also a player-piano." She stood and lifted the lid on the bench. Paper rolls were neatly stacked and printed with song titles.

"Super. All we have to do is put in a roll to pump out music every day."

"Please, not this morning." Julianne held a hand to her forehead. She sipped her coffee and watched me flop down in an easy chair. It faced a rock fireplace and shelves of books with worn covers. "I'd guess that chair was his favorite."

"It's huge." I snuggled into the soft cushions. My hands rested on over-stuffed arms so big I felt as small as a doll.

Julianne walked to a display case with glass doors. "These figurines are exquisitely carved, some I guess are from walrus tusks and others are jade."

"Were they made by Eskimos in the Arctic?" I jumped up for a closer look.

"No doubt."

On the coffee table was a decorated wooden box. I lifted the lid. It was half filled with cigars. "Lucky Lew smoked cigars." The discovery of this small fact I felt sure to be important. My stomach growled loudly.

"Hmm, I'd say you're hungry. Let's explore more after breakfast."

"Yes, every room." Following Julianne to the kitchen, I hesitated a moment at the sunbathed staircase. I could imagine Lucky Lew standing there ready for a bear hunt in laced-up boots. His red shirt would be open at the neck. Sunlight streaming in would make his black hair glisten.

"Tish," Julianne called to her daydreaming sister.

Breakfast was cold milk from the icebox and what was left from sympathetic neighbors. I smeared cornbread with wild raspberry jam. We ate fast since we could hardly wait to explore the house.

We agreed to do the main floor first. I

rushed to the room where Lucky Lew died and timidly twisted the glass doorknob. There before us was the portrait. I flinched at the stern eyes and tightly closed mouth. "He looks mean in that picture."

Julianne read the artist's name in the corner of the portrait. "I wonder if Sidney Lawrence intended this man to appear strong or ruthless."

"Look at his pinkie. He's wearing the gold-nugget ring that he put on your finger."

"That is it. This morning I notice an inscription on the inside rim of the ring. It says, 'Cleary 1913'."

"Isn't that the year Papa came home?"

"Yes, his last year in Alaska. Cleary was the name of their gold mine."

"Lucky Lew must have loved it a lot. I sure that's why he gave it to you for a wedding ring."

Julianne took her eyes from the portrait. "More likely it was only out of convenience. Still, it is nice to know the nugget came from the Papa's gold strike."

"I'll bet Lucky Lew spent gobs of time in this room. There could be hundreds of clues right here." I twirled around with my arms out.

Above us were spooky heads of dead animals. A huge polar bear rug covered one wall, its face in a furious snarl. A moose and caribou with incredibly large antlers stared vacantly into space, their bodiless heads hung just beneath the high ceiling beams. There were also the proud heads of a Dall sheep, a mountain goat, and a brown bear with its tongue painted red. I guessed the stuffed white birds were ptarmigan like the ones Slim told us about. A pair of them and a tiny ermine decorated the top of a gun cabinet that held half a dozen rifles.

"This is definitely a man's room," Julianne said.

I cringed at all the vacant eyes spying down on us. "It gives me the creeps. Maybe that's why Stella Malone divorced him and left here."

"That would be a very small reason." Julianne turned toward the door.

"Let's look in rooms upstairs." I was thinking we had seen the study, sitting room, dining room and foyer.

I skipped up the stairs and opened the door to the bedroom next to ours. It was a pretty guest room in bright yellow and white. There was a sitting alcove, a brick fireplace, an adjoining bath and, overlooking the driveway, was a small balcony. I jumped on the feather bed.

"I'm going to think about moving in here," I said when Julianne entered.

"You mean after you're convinced the house is not haunted?"

I threw a lacy pillow at my sister and fled the room.

The next door was mahogany with carved scrolls and hinges that squeaked. The room smelled musty as if it had been shut up a long time. I sang in a silly chant, "I can guess whose room this one was."

"The room is as dramatic as the former Mrs. Kelovich might be."

It was a suite of two rooms done in orchid and greens. I pulled back a dust cover on a chaise lounge and revealed paisley printed upholstery. Above a fireplace built of white rock was hung a large painting of wild iris. Drapes on the windows were flowered and the carpet was in bold purple hues.

I pulled open bureau drawers, looked in a chest, wardrobe and a closet. "Nothing. Everything's empty."

"The room was all shut up and not in use. I wonder why Lew left it untouched like this. What thoughts did he have as he passed by it every day?"

"Maybe she put a spell on it. Patrick said she's a witch." I fidgeted toward the door, impatient to be out of the reach of a witch. Julianne followed.

"Didn't little Patrick also say she's a fortune teller?"

"A fortune teller named Madame Urina." I pushed open the door to the next room.

No doubt this was Lucky Lew's bedroom. It was a single room, made cozy with warm colors of brown and orange. A cast-iron, coal-burning stove trimmed in gleaming nickel was in the center of the room. I flopped into a leather rocking chair next to a gramophone.

"Umm, this is real comfy." I rocked the chair with vigor. "I smell cigar smoke."

"This room would be snug on a forty below zero morning." Julianne's fingers ran along the frame of an oil painting on the wall. It was of a lonely, snowbound log cabin under blazing northern lights.

From the dresser, Julianne picked up a leather-bound Bible with pages edged in gold. The binding crackled when opened, which told me it may never had been read. A letter fluttered from it to the floor.

I jumped out of the rocker and picked up the letter. Julianne pulled two more envelopes from inside the Bible. "Now why would a man with a big, well-organized desk downstairs put letters here?"

"Maybe he was hiding them. They could be secret."

The handwriting on the envelopes was full of swirling capital letters. I read the return address on an envelope, "*S. Malone, 206 Van Ness #5, San Francisco, California.* The postmark is this year on March something."

"The ragged edges on these envelopes are tears made with a thumb and not with the ivory letter opener on his desk."

"It looks like Lucky Lew brought the letters up to his bedroom to read."

"Isn't that curious?" Julianne spread the envelopes on the rust-colored bedspread.

"Julianne, what are you waiting for? Read them."

She hesitated. "It feels like a breach of privacy."

"I'll do it." I picked up one postmarked January 16, 1925. "It says, '*Make it a double payment this time, My Dear, for a merrier New Year*'. The note is not even signed."

"Maybe it's a reference to an alimony payment," Julianne unfolded the letter dated in February and read, "*$5,000 immediately, Sweetheart. And come through fast or I'll send a very interesting telegraph wire to that certain party in Seattle.*"

"Gee whiz, do you think she means Papa?"

"Or it could refer to someone we don't know."

"I never did see any telegraph wire come to our home."

The third letter was stamped in March. Julianne read, "*Get my old room ready. I've decided to live a little closer to my benefactor. Should make you happy, Darling. No more of your precious Alaska dollars will go to those foreigners in Europe. Just like you always preach, it's coming back to your beloved wasteland.*"

"It didn't look like he got her old room ready." I pointed toward the room with all the furniture draped in dust covers.

"But Stella Malone did come back. Tish, these letters sound like Lew's ex-wife may have been blackmailing him."

"I wonder if he had a secret that he didn't want someone in Seattle to know about." I ran searching fingers inside each envelope, but there was nothing more.

"These letters are dated close to the time Papa received Lew's letter that said he wanted to marry me. I wonder if there is a connection."

"I always thought the reason Lucky Lew wrote that letter was because he felt so bad about Papa's dying."

"Maybe or maybe not that was the only reason."

"Julianne, isn't it really sad that Lucky Lew had to go and die too?"

Julianne wiped a tear from my cheek and held me close for a moment. The ache of losing Papa had a way of sweeping over me sometimes without warning. Now, the hurt was multiplied by two.

CHAPTER 14

Slim's Life

When Tilly arrived in early afternoon, I offered to help prepare the soup we would have for supper. She handed me a pair of tweezers. "I'm sure those sweet little fingers can pull pinfeathers out of a fresh-plucked chicken. When you're done, we'll drop it into the pot and let it boil the rest of the day."

When the chicken was in the pot, Tilly showed me how to wash hardened mud off beans that were shipped from California in a gunnysack. Once I had a colander of beans rinsed, she sent me to search for Slim because the soup needed potatoes from the root cellar.

I heard Slim before I saw him. A steel blade cracked into wood, shattering the silence of the morning. Wielding a hatchet with his one hand, he splintered kindling into random piles of fresh-scented wood.

He stopped, looked my way and took off his wide-brim straw hat. Snowy hair was damp from perspiration. A checkered handkerchief wiped droplets from his forehead.

"Why are you cutting more wood when there's so much already?" A mountain of neatly stacked kindling lined the length of the woodshed.

"Ain't nothing like hard work to get the thorny cockleburs of grief out of the hide."

I thought a moment about thorns in sticker bushes. Seeing the sorrow in his slumped shoulders, I understood. My eyes went watery. Slim felt the loss of Lucky Lew more than anyone.

"Here," he said handing me the hatchet. "You go ahead and try it."

I hesitated. My hands had never touched a hatchet before.

"Grip it with both your hands. Keep your eye on the log."

I squeezed my fingers around the wooden handle. It was extra warm where Slim had held it. The blade blinked in the sun. Slim placed a log upright on the chopping block and stood back. "Go ahead. Smash it to smithereens."

I raised the hatchet over my head and let it swing down into the log with a thud and there it stuck. With a grunt, I lifted log and hatchet together and smacked down with all my weight. The blade went deep into the wood. I smashed it again and again. With every thud my whole body vibrated. The final blow ended in a loud crunch. The log split in two.

"I did it!"

"Wasn't I right? You feel a mite better?"

"Yes, I think so." My hands still felt a tingling vibration from smacking the wood.

Slim hung the hatchet on nails that stuck out of the wall on the shed. He set about stacking the kindling in a neat row. I pitched in and worked beside him until the pieces were neatly stacked.

"Tilly said I should ask you for potatoes from the root cellar."

"Okay, the cellar's this way." Slim led me into a dark, cold area beneath the house. I rubbed a chill that hit my bare arms. Gradually, my eyes adjusted to the dim light. My nose adjusted to odd smells including cabbage, carrots, and potatoes. Slim struck a match and held it to a wick on a kerosene lantern. With the glass cylinder in place, it illuminated shelves of vegetables and endless jars of jelly. He pointed to a line of frost in the dirt wall and called it permafrost. He explained how the temperature in the cellar stayed the same summer or winter.

I felt like Slim could teach me more about important stuff than I learned in school last year.

Since I didn't bring a bowl to the cellar, we both carried handfuls of potatoes up to the kitchen. When we dumped them into the sink, Slim said "You gals ought to be off looking at the river on a nice day like today."

"Do you want to, Julianne?"

"Not right now. You two go ahead." Julianne gave the pump handle a couple of pulls and water splashed on the potatoes.

Slim and I went out into the sunny day. There was enough breeze to keep mosquitoes away. We got to the riverbank in time to watch a beaver scurry into a slough. With a splash and slap of its tail, it disappeared into a dammed-up pool.

"You ever gone fishin'?" Slim asked.

I shook my head. "Do you think I should?"

"Fishin' is peaceful, good for the soul."

"Like chopping wood?"

He grinned.

Without thinking, I asked the thing I was most curious about. "Slim, did you lose your hand working at the gold mine?"

"No, that happened a long time ago. Let's sit for a spell and I'll tell you all about it." We sat in a clearing where we caught the breeze and had a view of the water lazily flowing by.

"There was this landslide," he started and told me a long story of tragedy. My heart filled with sadness and admiration.

When his story ended, we sat in silence for a while before we walked back through the woods. Slim pointed out white berries that would ripen into wild raspberries and tiny cranberries that would be red and juicy after the first frost. I picked wild rose blossoms and delicate wild iris. At the house, I put them a jar of water.

At bedtime I told Julianne, "Slim is like a grandfather." We were sharing a bed another night with Raggedy Ann between us. I still was not ready for a room of my own.

"I like him too. He was surely Lew's closest friend."

"He told me how he lost his hand. It's so sad. A rockslide came down right on top of his wagon. He was thrown from the wagon but hit in the head and was unconscious for a long time. When he woke up, he found his wife crushed under tons of rock. She and their unborn baby were dead. He even had to shoot the horse because it had broken legs. His hand was torn up, and he was so long walking to town that the doctor had to cut it off."

"Did he tell you where this happened?"

"It was when he lived in Idaho. Afterward, he was so sad and miserable that he began to drink a lot of whiskey. One day he sobered up and decided to be a gold miner. He thought he could pan for gold with only one hand."

"Well, he's learned to do nearly everything with one hand. Slim is a courageous man." We talked some more about the tough things that had happened in Slim's life.

It was warm so we left the window open. Mosquitoes buzzed against the screen. We finally fell off to sleep with the brightness of the midnight sun behind gathering clouds.

I heard a noise. The mantel clock said fifteen minutes before five when I opened my eyes and listened to raindrops strike the gable over the window. Then I heard another noise and sat upright with a jolt that awoke Julianne.

"Did you hear that?" I whispered. "It's like a creaking on the stairs."

"Someone must be out there."

"Let's see." I slipped out of bed. Julianne followed.

I slowly turned the doorknob and we both peeked out. There, looming up the stairwell was the shadow of a man in a cowboy hat and long coat.

Shrieks echoed through the house as both Julianne and I screamed in unison. Boots stomped down the stairs, across the slate foyer floor and the front door slammed. The shadow had disappeared.

"What in blue blazes goin' on?" Slim yelled.

Julianne and I ran down the stairs to find Slim, a comical sight in long gray underwear buttoned from neck to crotch. His white hair was tufted up on one side. His feet were bare, toes turned up on the cold foyer floor.

"Someone was prowling around in here," Julianne said as we hurried downstairs.

"A man was coming right up the stairs. We saw his huge shadow."

"Looks like we might need to start lockin' doors," Slim sputtered.

"You mean they aren't locked?" Julianne shivered in her nightgown.

"Not in my lifetime. Never thought I'd have to in Fairbanks."

"Julianne, are you going to call the constable?" I trembled in time with my chattering teeth.

"We're not going to call anyone, we're going to lock the doors. Whoever it was is obviously a coward if one little scream can scare him off."

"That ain't no little scream I heard. I thought the Kaiser himself had landed." Slim slid the bolt on the big front door.

I followed him to the door. "Slim, what's the Kaiser?" I pushed the drape back enough to peek out the front window. All I saw was rain falling across the wide lawn.

"The German who started the Great World War. You were just a baby when his airplanes bombed cities in Europe."

I thought about the comparison of that to our screams. "Slim, you exaggerate." My bare feet were freezing.

"Looks as though our uninvited guest was interested in finding some sort of papers." Julianne pointed at the open study door. Papers were scattered over the desk, drawers pulled out and their contents heaped in piles on the floor.

"Or maybe...certain letters." I said.

"It's the most damn fool thing I ever heard tell of. But it sure ain't worth freezing my tail off for. You two best get into something warm too." Slim started off toward his quarters calling back, "Guess it ain't too early for coffee. I'll be gettin' the kitchen stove fired up."

"Let's get those letters and show Slim," I said.

Julianne nodded. "Maybe he can shed some light on just what they mean."

CHAPTER 15

The Funeral

The graveside service was in the late afternoon. Overhead clouds threatened thunder showers and darkened gravestones and wooden markers. The water of the Chena River reflected a solemn gray. Moist air was pungent with the scent of moss, muskeg and fresh-shoveled dirt.

"The murderer is sure be here, Julianne," I whispered. She nodded and straightened the collar on my sailor dress that she insisted I wear. She was in a light gray skirt and white blouse with a black ribbon tied at her neck.

Standing in the grass with us were Slim, Alice and her family, and Tilly Waters with her husband. Tilly called to Emmy Petrokov, who had all six of her children with her. We were introduced and she agreed to continue being the house cleaner. About a hundred people surrounded the priest from St. Matthew's Church. I recognized Constable Dole, Judge Wickersham and Attorney Steven Mills.

Patrick tugged at my arm. "Tish, there she is. That lady hiding behind the black veil is Madame Urina. She's the witch!"

"Patrick, do not point. Remember your manners," Mrs. Allen reminded him.

"So that's the fortune teller." In a dress cinched tight at the waist, the woman was in black from veil to shoes. She returned our stares.

To be secretive, Alice put a hand over her mouth. The bodice of her pale blue dress heaved with puffs of excited breath. "And she's the former Mrs. Kelovich."

"Known as Stella Malone," Julianne said.

A handsome young man stood beside the mysterious Madame Urina. There was a strong resemblance in the two, hair and eyes as dark and glistening as coal. He was suave in a tailored suit, brocade vest and crisp bowler hat. He stood out among the other men, who all wore Sunday suits that showed the sheen of long wear.

A very different sort of man was on the left side of Stella Malone. Though he was young too, his shoulders slumped under a rumpled sport coat. His boots were scuffed, and his dry, uncombed hair was held down by a slouched hat.

Julianne gestured at the shabbier man next to the fortune teller. "That one might have been on the steamship."

"That's him! I'm sure he was the one who threw you on the deck," I said breathlessly.

"Which one?" Alice asked as her eyes urgently swept the crowd.

"The unsavory one next to the ex Mrs. Kelovich, Madame Urina, Stella Malone, or whatever she calls herself," Julianne said.

Patrick poked his head between Alice and me. "He's the one who did what?" His voice was well above a whisper.

Alice tugged on his arm.

With a frown, Mrs. Allen placed her hand over his mouth.

The priest began the service with everyone standing. After prayers and a Bible reading, Mayor Collins stepped forward. He unfolded a paper, cleared his throat and read words that praised Lucky Lew for service to the town.

As many eyes were on the widow as on

the mayor. Stares at Julianne were curious but not unkind, except for one. Stella Malone glared. My hand was on Julianne's arm and I could feel her tremble slightly. Although to everyone else I'm sure she looked as composed as the portly mayor.

"Lewiston T. Kelovich was a man this town will long remember. May he rest in peace," the mayor concluded. In two seconds the crowd turned into a sea of voices. People turned to one another and tongues wagged. Alice's parents drifted into conversations with many people. Patrick chased after a little girl in pigtails.

"Look who shows up when the show's over," Alice said with a beaming smile. "Doesn't he look like a college preppie in that tie and sweater?"

Leif Bjorgam parked a bicycle against a tree at the edge of the graveyard. He strode along the path to where we stood and took off his brimmed straw hat. "May I offer my condolences?" He patted my shoulder and reached out to shake hands with Julianne. "Sorry I couldn't get here sooner."

"It's thoughtful that you came." Julianne's black-gloved hand lingered in his. Alice nudged her. "Oh, you remember Alice, and here are her parents, Mr. and Mrs. Allen."

Leif shook hands all around and answered questions about the new airplane. Then the Allens were quickly lured away by a friend.

"You should have been here," Alice exclaimed. "Why, Julianne and I shed buckets of tears, especially when Mayor Collins said all those wonderful things about Mr. Kelovich. He was certainly a good and noble person."

"He was a good person," I said.

Julianne frowned at Alice. "Neither you nor I shed tears."

I spouted, "We were busy trying to pick out his killer."

"His what?"

"Oh, Leif," Julianne said. "I'll tell you all about that later. At the reception, if you're coming."

"Sure, I plan to pedal on over there." Leif's square jaw tilted in a bewildered look.

"There's tons of terrific food from all the women in town," I said.

"Mother and I baked cookies until midnight," Alice said.

Patrick ran up and tugged on Julianne's hand. "Mr. Goodwin has the Tin Lizzy cranked up. Can I ride with you?"

"May I," His mother corrected him.

"Not today, Patrick." Mr. Allen interrupted his conversation with a friend.

Julianne patted the boy on his back. "Another time we'll go for a long drive in the car."

Patrick pouted as Alice took his hand and told him to count the wooden crosses that marked graves while they followed their parents to the parked wagon.

As people left, they past by us and one by one offered words of sympathy. Both Julianne and I encouraged them to attend the wake. I watched each face for any suspicious looks that showed the slightest guilt, but none did. Stella Malone did not come by. She vanished immediately after the service.

Leif hung around until Julianne and I were ready to meet Slim at the Ford. Then he took off on his bike.

As we bumped along the rutted road, we could talk about nothing but the mysterious threesome. Slim identified the two young men with Stella Malone as her sons. He said the well-dressed one was Victor and the other was Hector.

"Julianne, I'm positive it was Hector who attacked you on the ship."

Julianne nodded. "I'm almost certain too."

"I saw Stella giving you the evil eye like only she can do," Slim said. "Only human being I ever saw who could put fear into Lucky."

"Why was he afraid of her, Slim?" I asked.

Julianne turned the Ford onto Lacey Street. "Surely he didn't believe Madame Urina has magical powers."

Slim combed his fingers through his beard in a slow, thoughtful way. "Lucky wasn't one to take much stock in hokey-pokey stuff, but once he told me it was a spell that caused him to marry her."

"Maybe she put a love potion in his drink," I joked but no one laughed.

"If so, the potion wore off real fast. Stella had highfalutin ideas that Lucky didn't cotton to."

"Ideas like what?" I asked.

"You can tell from those letters you found, she was hell-bent on traveling to Paris and them fancy places. She spent Lew's money quicker than gold can be dug out of the ground."

Slim stopped talking too soon. I ached to hear more, but Julianne drove the Ford onto the tree-lined driveway. Other automobiles, wagons and bicycles pulled in behind us.

CHAPTER 16

Townspeople Tales

Delicious food scented the house. Tilly had seen to it that Emmy and her two daughters got there immediately after the service. They put hot platters of baked salmon and roasted caribou on the dining table next to sliced wild cranberry bread, wild blueberry tarts, chocolate cookies, strips of smoked salmon, cheese and pilot-bread crackers. On the sideboard a tall, brass samovar was filled with hot, orange-spice Russian tea. Hot coffee was in an ornate silver service. From Lucky Lew's cellar, Slim brought up bottles of Irish whiskey. He said it was for men to add kick to their coffee.

I stood beside Julianne to help greet each guest. Leif and the lawyer, Steven Mills, stayed with us to introduce people. Nearly everyone had a story about Lucky Lew and we listened eagerly for clues.

Steven introduced a distinguished looking gentleman as the owner of a furniture store who said, "Lucky Lew was the shrewdest businessman I ever knew."

"He was a peace-loving man," said a lady who brought in a plate of tarts that she said were made with canned apples. Her husband with a cherry-red nose disagreed. Batting the air with his fist, he said, "That man loved a good fight, could punch like hell too."

The priest commented, "Lewiston was a generous contributor to the church and to the hospital."

"Best damn miner around. He could smell out a vein. Riley will attest to that. I'm surprised Riley didn't show up today," said Bud Quinton, one of the men who found Lucky Lew in the Bearcat's wreckage. Julianne questioned him, but he did not add more to what we had seen at the crash site.

Not one person called my sister Mrs. Kelovich. Everyone called her Julianne and me Matisha. They hit us with question after question.

"What will you do now, my dear?" the constable's wife asked. "Surely you and your little sister will go back *Outside*?"

Leif saw my look of surprise and explained that anywhere beyond Alaska was called *Outside.* Everyone around looked amused by my ignorance of their ways.

"We have no such plans, Mrs. Dole," Julianne told the woman, who was as thin as the constable was not.

Before Mrs. Dole moved off toward a group of ladies waiting to hear tidbits, she warned, "Living in the Far North is very different than in the Lower 48. Much more difficult, my dears."

Steven introduced Tony Otis as being in the business of delivering ice to businesses and homes all over town. "I hear Jonsey was your Pa," the jovial man said. "He and me spent a few months up-river on the Porcupine once. Brought in a few bags of dust too, by golly. He was a fine partner, your Pa."

"I'd love to hear all about your time together." I took on a real liking to this man.

Julianne echoed my feelings. "We would like you and Mrs. Otis to come to dinner sometime soon."

After an eon of mostly tiresome conversations, I escaped to the kitchen. My head was in a spin with all the questions about school in Seattle, the trip up the Inside Passage and the flight from Seward. In the kitchen Emmy's daughters asked me the same questions, but with them it was fun to answer.

Helen was a year older than me, and Sissy a year younger.

"Tell us about Seattle," Helen pleaded with her brown eyes shining. "I just can't imagine what a big city is like."

"Is it true everyone there has a Ford car?" Sissy asked. She looked cute in her cotton kuspuk, a Native-style pullover dress, trimmed in yellow rickrack.

I told her some people had automobiles. I tried to describe the ships in the harbor, the many schools, different kinds of stores, and all kinds of houses, but I don't think I gave them a good picture of Seattle. I was glad to give up when Tilly bustled into the kitchen.

"Tish, your sister needs you back in the living room." She filled a platter with cookies and handed it to me. "Please put this on the dining table."

As I started to weave my way through the crowd, Alice gaily grabbed the platter out of my hands. "I'll pass them around for you." Her gaze swept past me and settled on Steven Mills.

The lawyer was still standing with Julianne. I tagged after Alice as she waltzed breezily across the room to Julianne's side. Julianne introduced her to Steven.

"So delighted to meet you."

"I'm pleased to meet you, Miss Allen. You must be new in town." Steven took a cookie from the tray with his eyes on her pretty face. Without the pillbox hat Alice wore at the funeral, her shimmering blond curls bobbed playfully around rosy cheeks.

"Mr. Mills is the lawyer for the Lucky Lew estate," I said. "He promises to read the will on Monday morning." Julianne gave me with a glare that could only mean I should shut up about the will.

Alice fluttered her long lashes."I've just arrived from Seattle and I'm planning to become a real sourdough. Although I don't know how I'll manage to learn all I need to know about living in Alaska."

"If I can be of any assistance....."

"How super! A smart man like yourself would be so much help."

I covered my mouth to hold back a giggle as Steven escorted Alice to the refreshment table. Later, it was no surprise he offered to walk her home. They left together.

It was late in the afternoon when the last guests drifted away. I was outdoors into a game of hopscotch with Sissy when Julianne and Leif strolled onto the long porch.

The air was fragrant with the blossoms of sweet peas that climbed to the railing around the porch. Colorful nasturtiums and marigolds were showy in the flowerbeds. White, puffy clouds drifted across the deep blue sky.

I intentionally hopped on a line and announced, "Looks like you win, Sissy."

"I did, I won." She squealed with glee. "But I better go help before Mama calls me again."

She ran into the house and I wandered up onto the porch. I was too curious to leave Julianne and Leif in a private conversation. They stood next to the railing covered with fragrant flowers.

"I can see why you love flying, Leif."

I butted in. "It's so exciting."

Leif grinned at me and gave me a good pal pat on my back.

Julianne continued, "Not only for the thrill of flying through clouds, but the industry as a whole is truly an exciting challenge. To be a part of that is something good."

"How about you. Are you looking for a challenge?" Leif said.

"Actually, I am. Contrary to popular belief, I came to Fairbanks not to marry, but to pursue some sort of career."

"We thought Lucky Lew would help Julianne find a job." I crossed my fingers for fudging since I had never had such a thought.

"What about the inheritance? You shouldn't have to work. He was a rich man."

I was ready to agree, but held my tongue.

"I don't know what will happen with his estate, or even if Tish and I have any right to a penny of it. It'll be months, I suppose, before all that is worked out. Meanwhile, I'm going ahead with my plan to work at something."

"Well then, would you consider holding down the office at the hangar?" Leif asked. "We need someone for only a few hours a day until we get more contracts."

I jumped up and clapped my hands. "Julianne, you have a career!"

Julianne's face lit up. "You're offering me a job working at the airfield with you and Jess?"

"I warn you, the pay is low. But we sure could use the help."

"When does she start?" I asked before Julianne could speak. I was thrilled to think we would have a link to the airplanes.

"How about a week from Monday?" He grinned and his blue eyes twinkled.

"Super!" I answered.

"Thank you, Leif." Julianne gave his hand a squeeze.

"Does this mean you two won't be going back to Seattle anytime soon?"

"We're staying!" I nearly shouted.

"Actually we don't have anywhere else we prefer to go." Julianne turned from leaning on the railing and sat down on the white rocking settee. "Besides, we both want to find out who is responsible for Lew's death."

Leif's eyebrows rose. "Responsible?"

"The car wreck was no accident, Leif," I said.

He gave me a doubtful smirk.

Julianne explained how we had found the cut cable and we both told him about the threats on board the *Northwestern*.

He frowned. "So that's why you three gals said the train trip might not be safe. I've been wondering about that. Looks like someone wanted to prevent you from marrying Lucky Lew."

"Whatever the original purpose, now that Lew's dead and I'm here, no one is likely to threaten me."

"Except for the prowler who sneaked into the house," I said.

"What?"

"Now Tish and I make sure the doors are locked every night. An intruder gave us a scare and rummaged through Lew's papers."

"We screamed and scared him away," I bragged.

Leif sat down next to Julianne. "I don't like you two alone in this big house."

"Thanks for the concern, but Tish and I are fine here. We have Slim with us."

"Slim is really nice," I said.

Leif shook his head slowly. "An old man with one hand?"

"He is remarkable." Julianne sighed. She held his gaze for a moment.

It was a moment that lasted so long that I forced a little cough.

Leif jumped to his feet as if sitting next to Julianne might be dangerous. He took out his pocket watch. "If anything like that happens again, promise you'll call. Ask the operator for 407J. That's the hangar." He opened the cover on his watch. "I've got a short hop in an hour."

Julianne stood up and brushed her hands over her skirt. "You're likely to be thousands of feet in the sky any time we're in peril."

"Call the hangar anytime. I'll tell Jess to come running."

"We promise," I assured him.

When Leif climbed onto his bike, he called back to Julianne, "I'll see you a week from Monday, nine A.M."

Julianne smiled. "I'll be there."

I hugged my sister. "I'm glad you have a job, Julianne."

"Me too." She smiled. Her eyes were greener than ever as she watched Leif and his bike disappear beyond the trees.

CHAPTER 17

Last Will and Testament

The offices of Collins and Mills, Attorneys-at-Law, were on Second Avenue, above the Model Cafe. At ten o'clock Monday morning, after walking to town in the summer sun, Julianne, Slim and I climbed the steep, narrow flight of stairs. The café made the air pungent with the scent of the morning's bacon and fried potatoes. I pinched my nose.

Julianne pressed a hand on her stomach. "Those odors do make the business at hand even more unsettling."

Slim paused on the stairwell landing. "Now that's a climb to take the wind out of a body."

Three doors lined the hallway on one wall. Windows on the other side let in bright light and heat from the summer sun. The glass on the door at the end of the hall was engraved

with gold-edged letters, "Collins and Mills".
Before we reached it, the door sprang open.

"Oh good, it _is_ you I heard," a flustered
Steven Mills said. "I mean to say, it's good to
see you. Good morning, Mr. Goodwin,
ah....Miss Dushan.... er.... Kelovich, and ah...
Matisha."

"Hello, Mr. Mills," I said and brushed by
him as he swung the door wide for my sister
and Slim. Just two steps inside the office, I
froze. The attorney's jangled nerves were
explained in full. We were face to face with
Stella Malone and one of her sons.

With quick, halting words, Steven said,
"May I introduce Stella Malone and her son,
Victor Malone." He turned to the mother and
son. "Please meet Mrs. Julianne Dushan
Kelovich and her sister Matisha Dushan. I do
believe you know Slim Goodwin."

Julianne managed a toneless, "How do
you do?" I sealed my lips, glad to feel invisible
as stares and glares flew over my head.

Victor rose and extended a manicured
hand to Slim. The handshake was brief and
limp.

"Hmmm," said Stella Malone between red
painted lips. She remained seated with her chin
haughtily tilted up. Under a black satin, wide-
brimmed hat, her dark eyes were icy, yet

striking. She wore a snug-fitting, black dress as if she was in mourning, but it was cut so low over her bosom that I gulped wondering if flesh would tumble all the way out any minute.

Victor was dressed princely in his well-tailored suit. His black hair glistened with oil. He bowed politely to Julianne. "It is a pleasure to meet so fair a lady."

Julianne stiffly gave him an indifferent nod.

"Yes, well...," Steven Mills said with his ears and cheeks glowing red. "Please have a seat, ladies. Perhaps you would like to pull up chairs too, Mr. Goodwin and Mr. Malone."

We all sat down in chairs that faced the attorney's desk. Steven seated himself behind it and shuffled papers. He cleared his throat. "Ladies and gentlemen, the dearly departed, one Lewiston T. Kelovich, has left in the trust of this law firm two documents comprising his last will and testament. The first one I will read was drawn up five years ago on July 31, 1920."

He threw a fleetingly glance at Stella Malone then us. "You will notice it is worded in general terms, stating relationships rather than the names of individuals."

Hunching over the typed document, he read, "I, Lewiston T. Kelovich, bequeath to my trusted friend and butler a monthly salary for his lifetime, plus the Salcha River property. The remainder of my estate I leave to my surviving spouse." He then held up another paper written in ink by an unsteady hand. "This is dated June 14, 1925, two days before death overcame Lewiston T. Kelovich."

"Really?" Stella Malone spit out that word. Her breath came so hard that her exposed bosom heaved up and down.

Steven cleared his throat but did not lift his eyes from the paper. He continued to read, "This will is to supersede any and all prior wills. Hereafter, I, Lewiston T. Kelovich, leave to Calvin Slim Goodwin the fishing cabin on the Salcha River with the ten acres it sits on, plus his usual salary for his lifetime. To Tim Riley, in memory of his son who died in my employ, I leave the sum of twelve thousand dollars. All my remaining possessions, property and holdings I leave to my surviving wife, Julianne Dushan Kelovich, with the provision that all her investments remain within the boundaries of the Territory of Alaska."

"Poppycock!" Stella Malone declared.

He held up the document. "As you can see, the signatures on this document are that of Lewiston Terrence Kelovich and witnessed by Judge Wickersham, Doctor Noble and myself."

High heels on the lady in black slammed onto the hardwood floor as she sprang off her chair. "That scribbled piece of paper is a fraud. The bunch of you cooked up this scheme with that gold digger to cheat me out of what is due me." A flame-red fingernail jabbed at Julianne.

"Mother." Victor impatiently put his hand on the arm pointing at Julianne, but she pulled away.

"Look at that handwriting. That's not Lew's writing. I'll testify to that in court." She slammed her fist on the desk so hard that the inkbottle jumped in its well.

Steven clutched the document to his chest with his eyes as wide open as the famous actor, Eddie Cantor. "Judge Wickersham will assure you of its authenticity."

"I'm the only wife Lew ever had. I'm his only heir," Stella Malone shouted. She twirled around to Julianne, her dark eyes blazing. "No teenage hussy is going to come breezing into town at the last minute to take it all away. Do you understand that, Miss Dushan?"

"You leave my sister alone." I jumped up so fast that my chair crashed to the floor. I scooted to Julianne's side.

Julianne patted my hand but did not reply to Stella Malone.

171

"Stella," Slim said in his slow drawl "You got all you're ever gettin' out of Lucky Lew."

"You... you... interfering old geezer. When this thing is settled, I'll see to it you're kicked out on the street.

"Mother, isn't this best discussed first with our attorney?" Victor spoke through clenched teeth. He righted my chair, crossed to the door, and held it open.

Stella took a step to the door then paused. "Mills, I'll see you in court where I'll get you disbarred for the shyster you are."

Sharp heels hammered through the hall, pounding down the long staircase. She was gone, but the scent of strong perfume lingered making her rage feel as alive as ever.

"Phew!" I squeezed a hand over my nose.

"Let's have some fresh air," Steven said. He pushed up the window that gave a narrow view between buildings along the Chena River. "That is one strange woman."

"I hope she calms down soon," Julianne said with a look of shock.

"When she does, it's going to be a time to start worrying," Slim said with a far-away look in his gray eyes.

Leaning over the windowsill, I could see

Stella Malone stomping on sidewalk boards as if nasty spiders were under her feet. I watched until she and Victor rounded the corner at the Anderson's Drugstore sign.

"Mrs. Malone is certainly not rational," Steven said. "When Mr. Kelovich became concerned about his failing health, he sent for me and asked me to review the old document."

Slim gave the hat he held a whack with a clenched fist. "Once Lucky told me that it was Stella who nagged him to write out a will. That was right after they married."

"Well, I warned him that since the first document did not designate recipients by name, his former wife may receive the inheritance. As his attorney, I encouraged him to make out this hand-written supplement. I had it typed up, but unfortunately, not in time for him to sign."

I bent over the desk to look at the papers. "What would have happened if we didn't get here in time and there was no wedding?"

"Mr. Kelovich was a stubborn man. He refused to consider that possibility until that last day. Then, he insisted on giving verbal testimony that, if he should die before the marriage, the estate should still go to the daughters of Jonah Dushan. The verbal will was duly witnessed by the doctor, myself and the judge." Steven shook his head. "Stella Malone would have had a heyday with that in court."

Julianne pressed both hands to her cheeks. "Then do you think she will actually contest the will?"

"You can bet on it," Slim said. "That woman will use every ounce of sorcery to put a whammy on the court and to get the judge thinking her way."

I moved to my sister's side. "She is a witch. Just like little Patrick says."

Julianne shook her head. "If it is her son Hector who implements all her whammies, I won't worry. So far, he hasn't been more of a threat than I can handle."

To Steven's confused look, I explained, "We are sure Hector is the one who cut cargo loose, pushed Julianne down on the ship, and sent her a mean note."

"What, he inflicted harm on you?"

Julianne and I took turns to fill him in on the details. "He's probably the man who broke into the house, too," I added.

Julianne nodded. "Someone entered the house Friday night and rifled through Lew's desk."

"He ran away when we screamed," I said.

Slim smirked. "That scream would scare the devil himself away."

"Hector Malone sounds like a dangerous man," Steven said sternly. "I understand he was doing jail time in Seattle up until a few months ago. It is conceivable that Mrs. Malone booked his passage on the ship you were on."

"Everybody in town knew Lucky was hurt bad, including Stella." Slim slapped his knee. "It'd be like Stella to send a telegraph wire to Hector and get him to do her dirty work."

Julianne stood up and took a deep breath. "Well, we can't let that woman take all the pleasure out of this beautiful day. Tish, let's explore the town."

CHAPTER 18

Walk Around Town

"Could we walk to Alice's house?" The idea excited me.

My excitement was contagious. Steven Mill's face lit up. "It's almost noon. I would be most delighted if you and Miss Alice Allen could possibly join me for lunch. The Model Café has a fine hot beef sandwich."

"That would be great. Shall we, Julianne?"

"Thank you, Steven. I'm certain Alice will be pleased too."

Hearing that felt as if sunshine had pierced through clouds. "How about you, Slim?"

Tired lines puckered his brow. "I'm going to head on back home. Maybe take a nap."

We left the attorney's office together. I skipped ahead. Down the hall there was an open door, and I peeked in. A woman inside pumped a treadle sewing machine. I froze in my tracks at the sight of her feet peddling and her hands guiding flowered cloth under a needle. It was as if my mother suddenly appeared.

Slim noticed how I stared into the room. "That there is Tamoko's Tailoring Shop, the best sewing woman to be found anywhere."

Julianne gently brushed a stray curl off my forehead. "Our mother had a seamstress shop. With hard work she grubstaked Father's quest until he struck gold."

"Lucky was a man full of envy over Yvonne Dushan. He called her a true saint."

"Mama always did sewing. She made me dresses with ruffles." I rubbed my eyes and sighed then ambled thoughtfully down the steep stairs.

On the sidewalk, Slim pulled on his brimmed hat, wished us well, and headed for the Ford to drive home.

The boardwalk creaked under our feet as we passed stores with false fronts. Posters in windows boasted of bargains to be had. A sign in Lavery's Grocery advertised butter for fifty cents a pound. Julianne winced. "That's twice what we pay in Seattle."

I pressed up to the window of Bloom's Hardware where merchandise of all kinds reached the rafters. Across the street, a steady stream of customers entered and left a public shower and laundry. Paint was peeling from its weathered boards. We passed two saloons, the post office, and a shop with men's overalls and ladies' hats in the window. People who passed by greeted us, saying hello and wishing us a good day.

"Do you think people know who we are?" I wondered.

"No doubt. I imagine we've been big news, Tish."

I pressed fingers dramatically to my forehead. "Maybe they're saying, 'Look, there goes Lucky Lew's young, deathbed bride and her poor little orphan sister'."

Julianne smiled at my antics. "Actually, I think the lady with twins and the shopkeeper, who swept the walk, really meant it when they wished us a good morning."

"Julianne, don't you think Fairbanks is beginning to feel like home?"

"Yes, I believe it is."

The boards of the walkway ended at the school grounds. We walked along a dirt path. Alice spotted us from the garden. She called and dropped a burlap sack. Green lettuce leaves sprinkled over the ground as she ran toward us. Her smiling face was smudged with dirt.

She greeted us with hugs and chattered rapidly. "You look worn out, Julianne. The whole morning with all that legal stuff had to be long and boring."

"It sure wasn't boring," I exclaimed.

"It was anything but," Julianne said. "We'll tell you all about it while you wash up. Steven Mills wants us to meet him for lunch."

"Oh, he invited me? That is just too terrific. He's just the spiffiest fellow."

"Gee whiz, Alice, I remember you said that same thing about a certain seaman," I teased.

Alice giggled. "You must think me a little bit fickle."

"Just a little bit, Alice." I winked at my sister.

Julianne laughed and her tired look vanished.

In the house we found Mrs. Allen in the kitchen. She greeted us with warm hugs and we told her of our lunch date. While Alice pumped the handle at the sink until cold water gushed into an enameled basin. She added hot water from a kettle and washed her face and arms.

"You're running off with that sack left out in the hot sun," Mrs. Allen complained.

"Oh gosh, I forgot." She rubbed her face in a towel.

"I'll bring it in." Julianne headed for the door. "You get dressed."

I helped Alice button the back of a snug yellow dress that flattered her round figure. "Do I look good enough to impress an attorney?"

"You sure do."

Julianne came through the screen door and set the bag of lettuce on the table.

"Thank you, Julianne." Mrs. Allen emptied the sack into a large metal colander.

As we walked at a good pace, Julianne said, "I was impressed with Steven today. He is a fine attorney."

"How exciting. A man on his way up." Alice gave that thought a big smile.

I began our tale. "You'll never guess who was there this morning, Alice."

Julianne said, "None other than Stella

Malone and her son Victor."

"Victor is the Rudolph Valentino son, not the hobo one." I pressed a finger above my lips to show a mustache.

Alice came to a stop. "What was that woman doing there?"

"Basically, she was there to inherit money." Julianne said.

"But she sure got fooled. Not a penny was left to her." I tugged on Alice's hand.

"No money at all?"

"None. She got so mad that she almost hit Julianne." We gave Alice details of the will as we neared the center of town.

"Stella Malone has threatened to contest the will," Julianne said.

"That means to get a judge to decide who gets the inheritance." I showed off my new knowledge.

"I've never seen anyone in a worse temper," Julianne said.

"Father told me she was arrested once in Dawson City for being a witch," Alice said in a near whisper as the boardwalk filled with people along the way.

"Holy smokes!" I did not whisper.

"He says there's a rumor that she bribed her way out of jail and left town in a hurry."

"Well, let's not let that woman ruin our appetite." Julianne led us across Second Avenue to the Model Cafe.

A bell on the door jingled when we entered. The long, narrow room was lined with a dozen tables. Each was covered with a white tablecloth and adorned with a vase of artificial flowers. Steven Mills jumped to his feet and hustled about pulling out chairs and seating each of us. His eyes focused mostly on just one. Obviously, he was enchanted with Alice as she plunged into rapid conversation about beauty school and her plans for being a lady barber.

I showed off my hair that Alice had bobbed, but mostly Julianne and I had little to say. We concentrated on bowls of the soup-of-the-day. As soon as we finished slices of cake, we left Alice for Steven to escort home if the dreamy couple ever stopped lingering over cups of coffee.

Around the corner, we say how the Chena River was flowing high from the late spring thaw. Dark clouds were building in the sky.

"I'll love to walk over the bridge." I ran

ahead. "Look there's the *Tanana Sternwheeler*."

Julianne followed me at a ladylike pace. The paddle–wheeler was being unloaded at the Northern Commercial Company dock. We leaned on wooden beams supporting the bridge. Below workers stacked up boxes.

Julianne watched in a thoughtful way. "Leif says that with the new railroad and airplanes, the time is coming when steamboats won't be needed anymore."

"Then we need to go for a ride on a steamship real soon." I waved at people gathered beneath us on the dock. "I'll bet Lucky Lew went on the Chena River a lot."

"I'm sure, on this river and bigger ones like the Tanana and the Yukon." Julianne and I dreamily watched swirling water rush under us.

A shout came from behind us. "Hey, lookie there!"

We turned toward a rundown hotel near the bridge. A man whose face was shaded under a slouching hat, swayed in the doorway.

"I'll be danged if it ain't the brand, spanking new widow lady," he yelled. He waved both his arms in a haphazard way.

"It's that scary Hector Malone."

"Watch your step there, little misses.

Both of you might tumble into the muddy river and the silt will pull you down, down, down." With an evil chuckle, he reeled about and disappeared into the hotel.

I grabbed onto Julianne. "He frightens me."

"That was just drunken babble. He's no real threat when he can hardly stand up."

"Since drinking alcohol is against the law, why doesn't he U.S. marshal break all the bottles of whiskey at that hotel." I was remembering the stories about prohibition in the Seattle newspaper.

Just then, a clap of thunder boomed across the heavens. We both flinched and held onto each other. A gust of wind swept down from purple clouds, blowing our hair and billowing our skirts.

Julianne gripped my hand. "Come on, let's get home before the rain starts."

Running to the end of the bridge, I didn't look down at the deep, muddy water. I looked up to the Virgin Mary statue that stared solemnly from the Catholic Church steeple. Spruce trees and swaying willow bushes lined the path along the riverbank. There were no houses on this side of the river. Across the river I could see the drug store, the Nordale Hotel and small shops. The tall arches of the bridge hid the dingy hotel that Hector Malone had staggered from.

Raindrops pelted us as the Kelovich mansion came into sight.

CHAPTER 19

The Past Revealed

"Julianne, how rich are we?" I asked while drying breakfast dishes.

Slim had the *Daily News-Miner* spread out on the kitchen table. He held a magnifying glass to help his old eyes read the newsprint.

Julianne gave a last rinse to the oatmeal pot. "I don't know. But, regardless of the amount, inheriting Lew's money does not make me feel comfortable."

"Well, it sure sounds like he wanted us to have it."

"Why? Why was he so determined to leave his estate to us?" She pulled the plug on the sink and soapy water drained away.

"Probably just so that witch wouldn't get it."

"Yet, why us? Slim, do you have any idea why he picked Tish and me to inherit?"

As if his eyes were glued to the newspaper, he did not look up.

"Slim knows everything about Lucky Lew." I let my dishtowel fall across the newspaper and leaned close to his face. His reluctant eyeballs came level with mine.

"Not everything. But there's one thing I know for sure." The legs on his chair squawked as he abruptly pushed away from the table. He hopped up and hustled to the back door. "It's high time I got them storm gutters cleaned out."

Julianne sighed. With a cloth, she wiped dust from the windowsill and watched Slim on the porch steps. "There is something he's not telling us."

"Gee whiz, why would he keep secrets from us?" I dried the last spoon and let it clang into the silverware drawer.

Julianne shrugged. "Loyalty to Lew, I suppose."

"I thought he was our friend." My lower lip pushed out.

"He is a friend, but it looks like we are on our own to search for clues. Today let's start with Lew's desk."

The study gave me chills. Fear and dread were in the room not only because Lucky Lew had died there, but the eyes of dead animals stared down from every wall. Also, there were the oil-painted eyes in the portrait of the hunter himself.

"Gosh, that painting gives me shivers. I think maybe Lucky Lew knows you're looking in his check register, Julianne."

"Then run along and pull chickweed from the flower boxes. I've never seen weeds grow as fast as they do here. It must be all the daylight."

"I'm staying. I want to be where the clues are." I snuggled up close to Julianne and peered at the ledger. Records in the leather-bound book were written in bold handwriting with a quill pen and blue ink. There was the date, amount, description and purpose for each check.

"Do you see any clues?"

"There are large checks written to *Cash*, so obviously Lew paid his miners in cash. But here's a curious one dated this year on January 24th. It's for $1,000 to Tim Riley and noted to be for *Donald's burial*."

"Isn't that the man who gets twelve

thousand dollars from the inheritance?"

"Yes. It's curious that none of the other mine workers inherit a thing."

"I'll ask Slim about that if he <u>ever</u> gets in a talking mood." I thought of how sweet he was when we sat on the riverbank together and he told me stories.

Julianne turned to a desk drawer crammed with file folders. I could see the folders were in alphabetical order with labels like Adams mortgage, Carson mortgage, and Delbert mortgage.

I found that boring, so I moved to a glass case that held pieces of carved ivory and jade. I rearranged the figures so sea mammals and seabirds were on one side and land animals were on the other. I decided I could spend hours in this miniature world of polar bears, walrus, puffins and Eskimo hunters. I picked up a perfect miniature of a dogsled team when a shriek from Julianne nearly made me drop it.

"What?" I yelled, barely managing to fumble the figurine back in place. I rushed over to the desk.

"How outrageous! These folders contain letters that plead for more time to make up past due payments." Julianne opened another file folder with the word *foreclose* scribbled across it. "Every folder contains a sad, hard–

luck story."

"Like what sad stories and what does foreclose mean?" I feel eager to hear the latest gossip.

"That means he has taken back property from people." Julianne pointed to the open folder. "This one had a death in the family." She picked up another folder. "This says Mr. Benson was injured and lost his job."

"Gosh, that sounds like really bad luck."

"I see no place with a hint that any of these stories touched the heart of the rich financier?"

"I hope Lucky Lew wasn't that mean."

"So do I." Julianne slammed the file drawer shut. She stomped into the hallway with a bewildered me at her heels. At the telephone she turned the crank on the wall box and pressed her mouth close to its speaker.

"102-B please," Julianne said to the operator. To me she said, "I'm calling Steven Mills."

With the earpiece dangling from a cord, she held it between us so I could hear too. We heard two short rings repeat then repeat again and again. The operator's voice came on. "Sorry, there is no answer. I think Mr. Mills is in court. You might try again in an hour or so."

Julianne thanked the telephone operator and impatiently slammed the earpiece onto the hook.

"You trying to break the fool thing?" Slim asked as he came in the front door. He flinched at our scowling faces. "What's the matter? You two been talking to Constable Dole again?"

"We made discoveries about Lucky Lew," I said. "And they're not good."

"Are you aware he made a habit of foreclosing on mortgages?" Julianne's tone was harsh.

Slim grunted, took off his hat and wiped a sleeve across his moist brow. He inhaled a big breath and let it out slowly. "Now, maybe if I had a cold root beer, I'd be willing to tell how all that came about."

"I'll chip some ice." I dashed into the kitchen and was glad to escape the rare sight of my sister's temper. I stood on a chair and lifted the lid on the icebox. With an ice pick, I struck fierce blows on a fresh block of ice that had been delivered that morning. Glasses were filled with ice chips by the time Slim uncorked bottles of yeasty root beer.

We sat at the table, each of us taking a sip of the sweet drink before Julianne spoke in a controlled, calm way. "Some of the letters I saw told of really hard luck. One was asking for only an extension of thirty days. But Lew refused, and every one of those people lost their property to him. Wasn't that ruthless?"

"He took their houses away," I added in a quiet voice.

"Now, now, some folks doubted Lucky was a reasonable guy, but he had his reasons. Those foreclosures were to keep Alaska money in Alaska."

"Meaning they kept the money in Lew's pocket?"

"Well, Julianne, he thought that was better than letting those people sell the property and take the money then go live it up Outside." Slim meant that everywhere beyond Alaska is *outside*.

I was thoroughly confused. "Why would he care where people take their money if it belongs to them?"

"He figured if it was earned here, it's got to stay here. Over the years, people mined out fortunes, then they escaped winters by high-tailing it to warmer climates. Lucky figured that cheats the Territory out of being prosperous."

"It sounds like his obsession hardened his heart." Julianne showed no hint of sympathy.

"I'm feared it kind of ended up that way." Slim raised his glass and took a long drink.

"Papa took all the gold he had to Seattle for us and Mama, but Lucky Lew liked <u>him</u> anyway. Right?"

"Lucky owed your daddy his life, and he never forgot that. Jonsey used to spout about taking gold back to you and your mother. That's when hot arguing started up. It was a thing they never agreed on."

"Apparently, Father won the argument," Julianne said. "He came home and bought us a nice place."

"He maybe done the right thing, but Jonsey sure didn't win no argument. Lucky saw to that."

"How do you mean?" I was sure Slim would tell us more.

The silver-haired man bit his lip. A long moment of silence passed with doubt dancing in his eyes.

"Slim, please tell us." Julianne rested a hand on his shoulder.

Slim slumped in his chair then raised his arms in surrender. "Come with me."

We followed his lanky frame that was bent over with the burden of the moment. He walked through the open double doors of the study. To avoid the portrait, his head was down until he stopped in front of the gun case. He reached up and felt along the top of it until his fingers found a key. With it, he unlocked the glass door and slid the butt of a shotgun to one side. Exposed was a combination lock.

"A secret vault." I thought it was just what Sherlock Holmes would expect.

"You might as well know the unlocking numbers. It's left then right to the numbers 1, 8, 6, 7. That's 1867, the year the U.S. bought Alaska from the Russians."

"How skookum! May I try to open it?"

"Go ahead."

The metal knob was cool to my fingers. I twisted the dial. Slim coached me with left and right turns. It ticked louder than a clock, one tick for each number.

"Now give the lever a yank."

I pulled and the safe clicked open. Brown envelopes were inside. Slim handed one to Julianne that was marked 'Cleary Mine'.

She unfolded a paper. "This is an assayer report dated April 21st, 1915."

"That's the report saying ore from the mine tests out real high."

Julianne unfolded another paper. "This deed and bill of sale from Father is dated nearly a month later."

"Your dad never saw that assayer report. If he had, Lucky would've been forced to cough up a quarter-million bucks and hand it over to him."

"Papa was cheated!" Tears popped into my eyes. "By someone he trusted more than anyone in the world."

"I'm thankful Father never knew he had been swindled." Julianne glared at the papers like they were biting bugs. "It would have hurt him so."

My tears trickled down and Slim put his handless arm around me. "Lucky didn't live easy with what he done. Sometimes he'd drink whiskey and get to talking about how he tried hard to get Jonsey to stay in the North. But Jonsey had a promise to keep to your mother so he had to go."

"Lucky Lew cheated Papa just because he was coming home to us?" I pulled away from Slim as if he was the traitor.

"Lucky never figured anyone should take more out of the territory than what they came here with," Slim rasped. "That's the way he saw things."

We stood together with words choked back. The papers were like loud, white screams dangling in Julianne's hands.

A new thought hit me hard enough to dry my eyes and free my throat. "So that's why Lucky Lew wanted Julianne and me here. He wanted us to have money he owed Papa."

Julianne shook her head in disgust. "No doubt it was a scheme to relieve his conscience. That way we would live off the wealth he swindled from our father."

Mean thoughts made my voice shake. "Then the fortune stays in Alaska with us. He had it all figured out."

Slim nodded and gazed sadly up at the portrait. In a quivery, gravel voice, he asked, "Can you promise me this ain't something the *Daily News-Miner* will get into print?"

Julianne put a caressing hand on his shoulder. "How much gets into print will depend on how far Stella Malone goes in contesting the will."

"Golly, everything is so different now." In my mind, I was opening a book and the story inside did not match the title at all. The title promised sunny beaches, but the story was full of fog, blizzards and ice storms.

"Things are different. Obviously, we do have a right to the estate after all." Julianne handed me a hanky.

"What about those people who lost their homes?" I wiped my nose.

"We'll just have to give those foreclosures a close look. Father would want any wrongs righted."

Over the next few days Julianne was absorbed in paperwork. I soon discovered I was no help to understand deeds and mortgages. I occupied myself with Slim in the garden one day and we went fishing in the Chena River on another. I caught nothing but did help fry the two grayling Slim caught. When Emmy Petrokov came to clean on Thursday, I joined Helen and Sissy in the chores of bed changing and dusting the furniture. We also pumped out songs on the player piano. We shared a pencil and tablet and played tic-tac-toe.

When Julianne was ready to discuss settlement of the estate, she called Steven Mills. To avoid the telephone party line, he agreed to come to the house. It was after supper when Julianne, Slim and I sat with the lawyer in the formal dining room.

With papers spread over the long table, Julianne began by saying, "Steven, since the

O'Connor foreclosure isn't final, I want us to buy them out, then resell the house. It sounds like they need the money they've invested in the house for medical expenses."

"I'm not sure I would advise that. Mr. Kelovich was explicit on the matter," Steven replied.

I spoke up. "Lucky Lew isn't in charge anymore. We are."

"At least until a court says otherwise, right?" Julianne added.

Steven nodded thoughtfully. "Please remember you are obliged to abide by his wish that money not leave the Territory."

"Steven, the plan is to buy the house back and it will be resold. Therefore money revolving around the house stays in Fairbanks."

"Hmm, an interesting point, Julianne. That sounds acceptable." A baffled expression washed over him.

"Good." I was so proud of my sister.

Slim smiled but wagged his head back and forth in disbelief.

Steven Mills attempted to answer all the questions Julianne fired at him. After a while she handed him a stack of files to review, then she asked about Timothy Riley.

"No one seems to know where he is. Since work stopped at the mine with the death of the owner, he's probably working at another mine. I will hold his check until he comes back to town."

"When he gets wind twelve thousand bucks is waitin' on him, he'll hightail it to town," Slim quipped.

"I hope he turns up soon. Since he and Bud Quinton both reported the accident, Riley might add more to what Bud told me after the funeral."

"Perhaps," Steven said. "But on another matter, I want to be sure you are aware of the 4th of July Ball the town holds every year."

"We heard all about it from Alice," I said.

"Oh, so Miss Alice Allen is aware. Then she has knowledge of it as well?" The eloquent lawyer stumbled over his tongue.

"I think she's just waiting for you to invite her." I flashed him a knowing look.

Steven Mills grinned and scooped up papers. As he left the house, his face matched the bright pink blossoms of wild roses that were thick throughout the woods.

CHAPTER 20

Victor Calls

Sunday evening was warm and without a breeze. Pungent smoke curled up from citronella pots on the veranda to keep mosquitoes away.

With scissors in her hand, Julianne confessed she was frustrated that all her research through Lucky Lew's files during the week had not disclosed clues that pointed to a murderer. "At least we can be certain of the secret he paid Stella Malone to keep quiet."

"That is sure to be the big secret Lucky Lew kept from Papa."

Slim puffed on a sweet-smelling pipe. "Yup, I think you girls hit the nail on the head. I'm bettin' Stella knew about that assayer report." White circles of pipe smoke coiled above his head and drifted among tall birch trees.

Julianne clipped purple wild iris blossoms that grew next to the steps and lined the driveway. "Although it does not seem likely Stella would want Lew dead. As long as he was alive, he would pay to keep her quiet."

"It's likely that Lucky stopped giving her pay after Jonsey died."

I held a vase of water while Julianne arranged the cut flowers. "I bet it was one of her mean sons that cut the car brakes."

"Well maybe, but..."

"Oh no! It could be the one who's coming this very minute." The vase slipped out of my hands. Water and flowers spilled down my skirt. "Maybe a killer."

Victor Malone approached, swept off his black derby and gave us a movie-star smile. "Good evening."

When he marched onto the porch, he bowed as if Julianne was Princess of the North. "I've come to apologize for our difference of opinion last Monday. My mother and I hope you will realize the strain we were under and find it in your heart to forgive."

I folded my arms firmly across my chest, not caring that a soggy wet skirt clung to my legs. Slim grunted, stood up and shuffled into the house. The screen door slammed. I would have followed but could not take my eyes off Victor Malone.

"I appreciate the gesture, Mr. Malone," Julianne said with exaggerated grace and seated herself on the settee.

"Please call me Victor. Here on the frontier, we don't go in for formality." He took a seat next to Julianne without being invited. "Is that lemonade you're drinking?"

"It is. Tish will be happy to fetch you a glass. Right, dear?"

I glared at my sister then turned my back and busied myself picking up the vase and spilled flowers.

Victor reached for the pitcher and filled the glass Slim had left behind. He took a thirsty gulp.

"It's a long walk from town." Julianne warily studied his black, restless eyes.

"How come you walked?" I barked rudely. "Don't you have a Ford car?"

"I'm not one to mix with the mechanical likes of an automobile. I did walk. I have mosquito bites to show for it." He scratched the back of his neck.

"Mosquitoes like cologne." I pretended to gag at the sugary-sweet scent of him that was stronger than the citronella smoke. Julianne gave me a watch-your-manners frown.

"As the sun gets lower, bugs become more fierce," she said. "It will be best if we escape indoors."

I couldn't see that the sun was any lower than it had been all day, but Victor jumped up and held the door open for us. We filed into the living room.

Julianne did not start polite small talk as she usually did with guests. Nor did she invite him to sit down. Instead we stood in the middle of the floor.

In the silence, Victor fidgeted by taking a few steps around the room. He glanced at pictures and a framed oval mirror on the wall. The sight of his handsome image in the mirror seemed to bolster him. His lips parted in a thin smile. "It's the talk of the town that a lady such as you, Julianne, would venture behind the steering wheel of one of those gas buggies."

"Julianne is a good driver." I set the vase of wild iris on a doily-covered end table.

"Did your mother send you here to discuss my driving?" Julianne was calm and composed. I could tell she took pleasure in his discomfort.

Victor responded with a nervous chuckle

and cleared his throat. "I come to apologize for my mother's outburst and to pay my respects to a very charming widow."

"And very rich," I snapped.

He stiffened and gave me a wooden smirk. "Your sister is much too beautiful for a man to stay away from for long."

"You've come here to flatter me, then?"

"And to entertain both of you ladies." Victor bowed like a man on a stage then he reached abruptly toward me. I backed away and fell into an armchair. His swift fingers touched my ear and he revealed a silver dollar in the palm of his hand. Then he made a silver dollar appear from my other ear.

"Wow." I giggled despite myself.

He smiled triumphantly. A gold tooth glinted from his mouth. He took a deck of cards from his pocket and fanned them accordion-like from hand to hand. He flashed them across the coffee table in front of me. "Pick a card."

I bent to the table and pulled the jack of hearts. He picked up the deck and told me to replace my card in the deck. Then he shuffled again, fluttering cards through the air. He pulled out a card and held it up.

"The jack of hearts. That's my card!" I was truly impressed. "How did you do that?"

"A secret of the trade." His gold tooth flashed again.

"What is your trade, Mr. Malone?" Julianne used a tone softer than before. She seated herself on the sofa.

"Friends call me Victor. Julianne, I want us to be friends."

"He's a gambler," Slim grumbled as he entered the room. He seated himself right next to Julianne, leaving no room for Victor on the sofa.

"In truth, I'm a gypsy of many trades."

"A true gypsy?" I was intrigued.

"My mother is Armenian." Kneeling at the low coffee table, he deftly dealt the cards in a solitaire game. "My father was Sicilian, though I never knew the man. I've learned everything from my mother, the marvelous Madame Urina."

"Can you read palms too?" I could not resist asking.

"I can, and hypnotize, and interpret the art of astrology." With amazing speed, he nimbly played out the cards in the solitaire game.

"Are both you and your brother followers of your mother's teachings?" Julianne's question sent a card fumbling from his fingers. The card landed at my feet.

"Hector, in truth, is my stepbrother."

I scooped the card off the floor. When I handed the queen of spades to him, our eyes met. "Your brother attacked Julianne when we were on the ship. We know it was him."

Victor stiffened. In a blink, he recovered and spoke rapidly. "I hope you are mistaken but, let me assure you, there is nothing to fear from Hector. I promise to speak to him. He will have me to answer for any offense against you."

"You tell that no-good bum he has me to answer to now," Slim snarled.

Victor scooped up the cards and stood up. He pulled a gold watch from a pocket in his satin vest, lifted its lid and said, "I must be off." Turning to me, he magically pulled a nickel from behind my ear. He placed it in my hand with a wink. "Thank you for the refreshment."

"Gee, thanks." I was awed, and turned the palms of my hands up to him. "Can you tell me what my palm says?"

"I will be happy to, but at another time. I must say good evening for now." Victor politely wished Slim a good evening and got a grunt for his trouble. Julianne and I walked with him to the door.

"I hope you will allow me to come again, very soon."

Julianne looked at him without a drop of kindness. "Victor, I am not at all interested in dating you."

"I can be patient for one so lovely."

"Good night, Mr. Malone," I said in an attempt to rescue my sister.

As soon as he bowed his way out, I shut the door.

"What was that varmint after?" Slim asked when we returned to the living room.

"He's after Julianne. He wants to marry her for money."

Julianne laughed. "If that's the best hex Madame Urina can come up with, we're pretty safe from the Malones."

"She don't give up easy." Slim combed fingers through his bushy beard as if pulling bits of memory from it.

"He sure knows a lot of tricks." I examined the nickel for clues of magic. "I can hardly wait to tell Helen and Sissy how he makes coins appear from nowhere."

"He's tricky, all right," Julianne said.

As the week went on, whenever I wasn't helping Tilly, Julianne or Slim with chores I practiced shuffling a deck of cards, but had no success making them fly from hand to hand the way Victor did. When Helen and Sissy came over, I tried guessing a card they picked from the deck, but I was never right.

My friends and I resorted to winding the gramophone in Lucky Lew's bedroom. We listened to scratchy voices that sang through a bell-shaped speaker. Music chimed from a spinning turntable. We sang and danced to the jumpy beat of *Oh Johnny, Oh Johnny* and *If You Knew Suzie*. Whenever the machine began to wind down, we exploded in laughter as recorded voices slowed and dragged out singing, "None sooo claa...ss...sy."

Sissy changed the cylinder and cranked the handle with her thin arms working hard.

Helen and Sissy were well up on town gossip and a favorite subject was Madame Urina. I did not tell them why I was so interested in the subject. I had promised Julianne I wouldn't discuss our search for the murderer with anyone. Since we were the only ones who believed Lucky Lew was murdered, it was better to keep it a secret. There was no need for everyone in town to think we were daft.

"Madame Urina is a gypsy," Helen whispered over the music, although there was no one to overhear us upstairs in Lucky Lew's bedroom. She stared at the dead man's leather rocker. Her almond eyes were wide open as if she could see more than an old chair there. "They say she can talk to dead people, talk to ghosts."

"You mean she does séances?" I lifted the needle off the gramophone cylinder so Al Jolson stopped singing *My Dear 'ol Swanee*.

"What's a séance?" Sissy asked.

"It's when everyone sits in a circle and the leader says magic words. Then spirits from the dead appear," I said, remembering an old Sarah Bernhardt film.

"How scary!" Sissy shrieked with her arms wrapped around her skinny body.

"I wonder if Madame Urina could call up Lucky Lew's ghost."

"I'm sure she could. If first, you give her money." Helen was full of teenage wisdom.

Later, when I shared this news with Julianne, she did not share my enthusiasm. "That is more trickery, Tish."

"What if spirits really can be called up? Gee whiz, Julianne, lots of people believe it's possible."

"I'm not one. Nor am I about to pay Stella Malone to prove the point."

Julianne threaded an embroidery needle. She sat in the bay window, making full use of the bright evening sun in the living room.

I was silent for a long moment, listening to the evening quiet. Rays of light streamed in from the low, lingering sun. "Do you think anyone could keep a secret from a ghost?"

With her mind on needlework, Julianne mumbled, "I would not expect so."

"Then, if we really could hear from Lucky Lew's spirit, he'd tell us right off who cut that brake cable. He'd say exactly who killed him."

"Tish, we'll find out. And we'll do it without talking to ghosts."

"Really? How?"

Julianne didn't have an answer, but she replied, "We just need to keep our eyes and ears open."

I pouted. "Starting tomorrow, you won't be seeing or hearing anything but airplanes."

"At least, I'll be starting my career. Even

though it's only for a few hours every morning."

Thinking about flying magically cheered me up. "Would Leif Bjorgam mind if I came with you, Julianne? It would be so nifty to see the hangar and the airplanes."

CHAPTER 21

An Invitation

As it turned out, Leif acted truly excited to see me, but he was struck shy with Julianne. He hardly spoke to her as she looked about the office. He laughed with me and welcomed my questions about his favorite subject, airplanes. He talked about the science of flight, how wind flows over and under the wing, pushing it up and sucking it up at the same time.

Leif grabbed my hand and trotted me out of the hangar to the airfield. The morning sun burst through a cloud cover. Signs of rain vanished in a gentle breeze.

"This is the Jenny." He slapped the side of an airplane smaller than the one we flew from Seward. "Want to hop aboard?"

"I'd love to." I almost sang.

He lifted me up onto the wing so I could

climb into the cockpit. The leather-scented seat was not cushioned and held me firmly at attention with the control panel before me. I had to scoot forward for my feet to reach the pedals.

"We use this plane mostly for lessons, joy-hops and stunts. It's the favorite of wing walkers." He beamed at me from the gravel runway.

When Julianne came up beside him, he jerked around as if a firecracker had just gone off.

She tugged on one of twelve struts that kept the wings joined together. "Even with so many wires to hang onto, I can't imagine anyone crazy enough to venture onto a wing while in flight."

"Did you ever walk on the wings, Leif?" I imagined him braced against the rush of air pressing him at hundreds of feet above the ground.

"No, I stick to flying from the cockpit. In my barnstorming days, I took a slew of walkers up." Leif glanced at Julianne and fidgeted like a self-conscious schoolboy.

I got his attention again by pointing at the panel of dials and gauges."Is this the compass that keeps you from getting lost?"

Leif stepped up on the wing and leaned in next to me. "The compass helps, but Alaska is so close to the magnetic pole that we have to correct for the extra pull."

Julianne ran her fingers over the bright lettering on the belly of the plane that read *Rainbow Flight Service.* "With such long distances between places, so many mountains, valleys, rivers, I don't see how that little compass can keep you from getting lost."

Leif stepped back onto the ground. He fixed his eyes on the company name in red letters and nodded. "Maps are scarce and not too accurate either. Sometimes we just have to trust instinct."

"And skill." Julianne smiled sweetly.

I leaned over the edge of the cockpit. "We both think you're a really good pilot, Leif. Flying with you was so great. I want to go again really, really soon."

"Thanks for the compliment." Leif's eyes were a merry blue as he glanced at me then lingered on Julianne.

"Leif, I came here to start my new job. Remember? Are you going to show me what you want done?"

Leif cleared his throat as if something had tried to choke him. "I think it'll be best if

Jess gives you a rundown on the paperwork."
He hesitated. "How about I get the Jenny
warmed up so your little sister can go up for a
spin?"

"Oh super! That's okay with you, isn't it,
Julianne?"

Her gaze flowed from him to me. "I
wonder which one of you wants to go up the
most. It's fine with me, Tish."

Leif reached up and lifted me to the
ground. "Wait in the hangar until you hear the
engine rev."

I gleefully took Julianne's hand and led
her out of the sunshine and into the cool
hangar. We found Jess Younker there dressed
in overalls and a mechanic's cap.

"I get to go on a hop with Leif, Mr.
Yonkers."

"Attagirl, you've got spunk," Jess said in
his gravel voice. He turned to Julianne. "Don't
worry, he'll take it easy with her."

We followed him into the cluttered office
that smelled of ink, dust and motor oil. The
floor was scuffed up and in need of mopping.
Julianne sat down on the business side of a
paper-strewn desk that was made of rough-
hewn wood. I was fascinated with all the
pictures of airplanes that covered the walls.

Only two photos were framed, others were tacked up and some were newspaper cutouts. There were maps, too, and an RC Cola calendar. It pictured a smiling beauty wearing red lipstick and white furs.

"Are you a pilot too, Mr. Younker?" I asked.

Jess pulled a rag from a pocket in his coveralls and rubbed grease off his rough hands. He poured hot coffee into two mugs."I fix them, not fly them. But Leif would spend 24 hours a day in a plane if he could."

"That doesn't surprise me," Julianne said.

"Golly, I sure don't blame him." I felt entranced with the airplane pictures papering the walls.

He chuckled. "With the way this business is growing, he may have to work mighty long days."

"You do look a little overwhelmed with paperwork." Julianne began to stack papers in various appropriate piles.

"Having you help is just what the doctor ordered," Jess said. "Our boss is on a freight run to Nome in the new Fokker. He's doing in one day what takes weeks by riverboat in summer or by dogsled after freeze up."

"Wow, that's fantastic." My appreciation of airplanes was growing more every minute.

"Quite a difference," Julianne said. "I'm amazed to learn how truly meaningful flying can be in Alaska where roads and the railway are very limited."

"By Jove, you're a lady who gets the whole picture." Jess chuckled again in his deep raspy voice.

"I'll be thrilled if I can be a part of something so exciting."

"In that case, let me show you all that needs to get done."

An engine roared to life, and I darted to the hangar office door. "That's the Jenny revving up," I shouted and left Jess saying words like *schedules* and *ledgers* to Julianne.

Leif took me up into the clouds and down over the river. We circled the town in a wide loop three whole times. As big black ravens swooped beside us, I knew I loved nothing more than being up in the Jenny airplane.

Over the next few weeks, I was invited to go to work with Julianne on Monday mornings. Leif took me for short hops and always explained how and why the airplane worked. I tried to memorize his every word. Flying was the best thing in my life.

As weeks went by, summer daylight grew shorter. Ducks, geese and cranes flew in from the Arctic. They rested on farmland, then began to fill the sky on their migration flights south. Toward the end of August, birch, cottonwood, and willow leaves took on brilliant fall colors.

There were times when Slim and I picked wild blueberries and raspberries that grew in wooded areas near the house. Helen and Sissy came over with their mother for housekeeping and we played games, and visited the library to check out books. Julianne was increasingly absorbed in her job at Rainbow Flight Service. I was at the field one morning a week, but she spent so much time there that I missed her. The murder investigation hit a standstill. No amount of research into Lucky Lew's files produced new clues.

I was anxious for school to start to fill up my time. It started the day after Labor Day when daytime and nighttime were nearly equal with light and dark. I hoped my twenty-seven classmates, who ranged from age six through eighth grade, would lead to new information. Several kids eagerly talked about Lucky Lew and Madame Urina when I asked, but said nothing that could be called a clue.

On a special day in the middle of

September, the house smelled of chocolate. Tilly baked a cake for Julianne's birthday. Alice came over to celebrate by trimming Julianne's long hair. Her scissors clicked away and bits of wavy, auburn hair fell to the floor.

I teased her by using a lock of her hair for a mustache and speaking as proper Mr. Sundborg. "Young lady, you are twenty years old. You must marry soon or become an old maid."

"Matisha, how can you say that about our precious Julianne who is a widow still," Tilly said as she smoothed frosting on three layers of chocolate cake. Her frown at me deepened when I dipped a finger in the rich frosting. It tasted even better than it smelled.

"Oh, Tilly, she is just pretending to be our father's attorney who put us on board the steamer in Seattle," Julianne said with a laugh.

"There's no reason to worry about being a widow with all the agreeable men around town," Alice said as she piled Julianne's hair up in a pompadour.

"Alice, I'm neither worried nor interested."

"I know someone who is." My first thought was a certain handsome pilot, but instead I said, "Victor Malone has come here to tell Julianne she is so beautiful."

"That man is amazingly annoying."
Julianne gave a few details about Victor's offers
to take her out for dinners and dancing.

Alice asked lots of questions about Victor
while she finished with Julianne's hair. Then
she did a good trim on mine. When Slim joined
us, we all gathered around the piano and sang
songs. We cut into the yummy chocolate cake
and sang *Happy Birthday* to Julianne.

September slipped away as fast as the
last migrating birds. Colorful fall leaves fell to
the ground. Wild cranberries turned deep red
and cooked up sweet and tangy with sugar. On
an October afternoon, when a heavy snow
storm hit, a knock at the door brought a
surprise.

"I got it," Slim called from the foyer, so I
continued to set the table for supper. He
brought a white envelope into the kitchen,
saying he left the delivery boy warming his
hands by the fireplace. "I hope that kid was
paid good to deliver this. He had to pedal his
bike hard as a race horse in that snow coming
down."

I grabbed the letter Slim held out. "It's
addressed to you, Julianne. The writing is real
fancy."

Julianne continued to stir gravy bubbling
in a skillet. "Go ahead and open it, Tish."

With a sniff I unfolded a sheet of embossed paper. "It smells like perfume." I read out loud,

> Dear Julianne,
>
> My son, Victor, has told me of his visits and how he is quite enchanted with you. He implores me to extend my personal apologies to you for the unfortunate incident of our last encounter. Hence, and because I want us to be warm friends, I most cordially invite you and your sister to join me for tea and cake this Sunday afternoon. I shall await your company at my home at three o'clock.
> Kindest regards,
> Stella Malone

Slim shook his head. "No good can come from going under that woman's roof. You'd best put a big 'No' on that letter and let the boy pedal it back to her."

Julianne took the note from me and reread it to herself.

"This could be our big chance, Julianne. We might get her to admit she's a blackmailer and trick her into giving us even more clues."

"You two ain't no match for Madame Urina when it comes to performing tricks. I'm warning, don't let her get her claws into you." Slim's thick brows pinched together.

"You both are right, I'm sure." Julianne slid the skillet off the hot burner. "However, if we do go, we'll need a witness. Someone else must go with us. That way, if Stella Malone reveals something significant, our story will be more credible."

Slim shook his head. "Don't look at me like that, Julianne. I won't be going within a country mile of that woman."

"How about our lawyer Steven Mills?" I asked.

"His presence would surely steel her defenses."

"How about our super friend Alice?"

"That's it, Tish. I'm sure Alice would appear harmless to her."

Slim rolled his eyes in a mocking way. "Now there's a witness any court would take seriously."

I ignored Slim's opinion of Alice. "Then let's do it!"

"We'll give the boy a reply and a good tip." Julianne dried her hands on a towel and pulled pen and paper from a drawer.

I climbed on a chair and reached into the coin jar on the shelf above the sink. In the note, Julianne accepted the invitation and wrote that our afternoon guest, Alice Allen, would be accompanying us.

I crossed my fingers. "Here's hoping Alice will go there with us."

"I'm sure she will." Julianne handed me the note.

When I took the note out to the boy in the foyer, I was surprised to see someone in my current events class at school. It was Charlie, an eighth grader with curly hair and a good smile. "Thanks, Tish," he said, looking at the coins I put in his glove.

"You're welcome." I realized those were the first words he ever said to me.

He pulled his knitted hat over a mass of deep brown curls. "Hey, Tish, that report you gave last week about airplanes was really good."

"Glad you think so, Charlie." I pulled open the door. "Be careful riding your bike in the snow."

He went out, climbed on his bike, and called back, "See you tomorrow."

It took me a second to remember he was

talking about school. "Oh, yeah," I called and thought I'd really like to see Charlie tomorrow. I waved before shutting the door.

In the hall, Julianne was on the telephone with Alice. She turned the earpiece so I could press close and listen.

"What if she puts a magic spell on you or some sort of voodoo?" Alice said. "It sounds dreadfully exciting."

"Slim says the Ford will make it through the snow just fine, so we'll come by your house to pick you up Sunday, a short time before three o'clock," Julianne said before hanging up. Then she spun around with a face gone pale. "Oh dear, what am I going to wear?"

"Something sophisticated." I described a mystical outfit with a big, flowered hat and veil.

CHAPTER 22

The Séance

On Sunday, Julianne brought the Ford to a stop in front of a painted sign that read *Madame Urina, Palmist.*

Our hostess greeted us graciously. Stella Malone was dressed in black and looked glamorous with her raven black hair swept up into a pompadour, lipstick redder than ripe tomatoes, earrings dangling the length of her neck, and rows of silver bracelets on both wrists. She pointed to hooks next to the door for our coats to hang on. With coats off, her dark eyes roamed over Julianne's lime–green flapper dress and matching cap that concealed her hair.

"Why Julianne, I see you've abandoned the black cloth of mourning in such a short time. How cheerful of you."

Julianne was saved from answering by

loud sneezes from Alice. Gardenia-scented smoke circled her way from a dish of burning incense. In between sneezes Alice managed to say, "Thank you for letting me join Julianne and Tish today, Mrs. Malone."

"Your home is very fragrant," I said handing Alice my hankie.

"I am aware that the children in this town think my home is a curiosity." Mascara-rimmed eyes glared down on me. "That is not surprising in such an unworldly population. It is a pleasure to be in the company of ladies who have not yet succumbed to a gold-camp mentality. My ears hunger to hear of the city, even one as quaint as Seattle."

"I like Fairbanks better than Seattle," I said and squeezed past her into the dimly lit parlor. A low ceiling and log walls made the room a cave of shadows.

"My dear child, you are so new to this wretched place." Stella's eyes narrowed to a squint. "You don't realize the new snow we have now in October will not melt until the end of April. The precious daylight we have today is shrinking rapidly. For the next half year, look forward to nothing but darkness, snow, ice and bitter cold."

I shivered. On the sofa, I snuggled in the middle between Julianne and Alice. The sofa was covered with a flowered and fringed shawl. Another flowered shawl covered the coffee table. The whole room was in shades of red, purple and green. Brass cherubs, glass knickknacks, and candles littered every shelf.

"Please make yourselves comfortable while I ready our tea." Stella swiftly disappeared behind a black drape.

We sat in polite silence sharing wide-eyed stares at the black drape. It was etched with the signs of the zodiac. Like the wall of a gypsy's tent, it formed a partition between the parlor and the rest of the house.

Stella reappeared with an ornate-silver tea service. Her red lips parted in a faint smile as she placed it before the sofa on a low coffee table. "Miss Allen, may I implore you to pour us each a cup?"

Alice blinked, then nodded and nodded again. With unsteady hands, she tilted the silver pot and half-filled fragile china cups.

Our hostess did not bother to thank Alice as she struck a match to light a candle on the tea service platter. The flame pulsated with nervous flickers reflecting off the silver. She moved across the room to light another candle.

I heaped sugar into my teacup. The tinkle, tinkle sound of a spoon stirred in my cup was all to be heard. No one spoke. Finally I asked, "Is this where you are a fortune teller and read the palms of people's hands?"

"Indeed it is. As soon as Victor arrives, I will give you a demonstration. Would you like that, Matisha?" She leaned into my face so close I thought rouge might rub off on me. I backed away.

"Oh, is Victor joining us?" Julianne asked and elegantly sipped her tea.

"He would not miss your company. Every single, young lady in town hopes he will call, yet he disappoints them. I believe he has become quite smitten with only you, Julianne." Stella's voice oozed as if coated with a sugary syrup. She settled onto a chair across from us.

"Mrs. Malone, I find men plentiful in Fairbanks," Alice said. "They are quick to complain of the shortage of unmarried ladies."

"Ah, but one young man has found you, I hear. Mr. Mills, the attorney. Do tell, is it serious with the two of you?" Stella's manner was firm and demanding.

Alice flushed bright pink. Before she could catch her breath, Julianne spoke up. "To Victor I made myself as clear as possible when I refused his invitation to the Harvest Ball last Saturday night. I'm not in the least, interested in his courting."

Stella's lips tightened. "Victor warned me you are outspoken. I beg you not to take your anger at me out on my son. I wanted you to come today to tell you I will not be contesting Lewiston's will, even though his passing is a great loss to me."

"I'm sure that will be a wise decision in light of the letters you wrote from San Francisco." Julianne spoke in a calm voice, but I felt her stiffen as did Alice and me with tension mounting. "Tell me, did the threat you held over Lew's head have anything to do with my father?"

Stella whirled out of her chair. The rush of air extinguished the candle on the coffee table. "How dare you insinuate..."

The front door slammed. A fog of cold air swept in preceding Victor Malone. "Mother, I'm here."

I could see him sling his snow-saturated coat and hat on a hook and smooth his oiled hair before an ornate wall mirror. His shiny shoes waltzed him in. "Julianne, Tish, and Miss Allen. It is a delight to see you here."

"Excuse me," Stella muttered stiffly. "I'll get shortbread from the kitchen." She bustled out beyond the curtain.

"Please pardon Mother if she seems a bit upset. Since Lew's death, she has been on edge. Despite the divorce, she was very fond of him."

The way Julianne insinuated with such a fighting spirit made me feel bold enough to ask, "Does Madame Urina know how to do a séance? One that could bring Lucky Lew back from the dead?"

"Tish!" Julianne clearly did not appreciate my effort to find clues.

Alice gasped and her hand gripped my arm.

A grin slid across Victor's perfectly sculpted face. He tilted his head. "That's quite all right. Actually, Julianne, I am surprised Tish mentions such a possibility. You see, Mother has done exactly that."

"She already did it?" I tugged from Alice's grip and slipped to the edge of the sofa until my feet touched the floor.

Victor nodded slowly. "Not a week ago, on the night of the full moon, she was successful in reaching out to Lew Kelovich. Why, the result was what prompted her to drop the legal suit."

"Hmmm." Julianne's arms were firmly crossed.

"Are you saying the spirit of a dead man

actually spoke to you?" Alice asked with her eyes rapidly blinking.

"Oh, yes indeed."

"What did he say, Victor?" The dark expression in his eyes held me spellbound.

"Well, Matisha, Lew pleaded for peace in his family." Victor's head spun around to his mother as she carried a plate of cookies into the room.

I grabbed a cookie as soon as the plate hit the coffee table and tried out my most buttering-up voice. "Thank you so much, Mrs. Malone."

Victor put a hand on his mother's back, caressing her gently. "Mother, the ladies are intrigued by the séance we experienced at the last full moon."

"Oh? Well, I must confess it was an exhausting experience." Stella's breathing began in hard puffs, as if she had run up a hill. She perched on the edge of a chair facing us.

"Could you do it again? Like right now?" I asked. "It would be exciting to hear Lucky Lew's spirit speak."

Julianne calmly sipped from her tea cup, but Alice gulped. I turned to see her mouth hanging open and her eyes like two full moons.

Mother and son confidently exchanged glances as if using mental telepathy, each reading the thoughts of the other. Stella turned her gaze to the ceiling. Her voice took on a distant quality as if she was talking from far away. "It would be difficult with the moon in decline. I believe a quarter of it has darkened since the last séance."

Victor spread out his arms in exaggerated reverence. "Mother, remember that time in Paris, you were able to call upon a spirit under a new moon. You gave a grieving widower wondrous comfort."

"Ah, remember that spirit was uniquely willing. The spirit of Lewiston Kelovich may be reluctant."

"I'll be glad to pay you if Tish wants you to try," Julianne said coolly. She avoided Alice's astonished glare.

"Oh, I sure do!" I squeezed Julianne's hand. Alice fidgeted so I grabbed her hand too.

"There will be absolutely no charge, Julianne. Although, I'm afraid no guarantee either," Victor said. "Mother, do you feel up to trying?"

Stella drew in a slow, grand breath and closed her violet-painted eyelids. "If you insist, with all my strength, an attempt shall be made."

"Then it will be done," Victor said as if announcing a show to begin.

Stella remained seated in a trance–like pose while Victor hustled about. He disappeared behind the zodiac drape. I could hear him oddly mumbling to himself. We sat still and waited. Julianne sipped more tea. I ate another crumbly cookie. Alice squeezed my hand.

Victor returned, cleared away the tea service, relit the candle, and closed the curtain on the room's only window. He placed four pillows on the floor around the coffee table.

"Please, everyone, sit on a cushion with your palms down upon the table." Victor's jaw was rigid. His fine features were distorted by shadows from the glowing candle giving him an evil look. "Maintain complete silence, please. Even your breath must not be heard."

I swallowed a last crumb and sat on a pillow across from Alice. Victor ceremoniously offered his arm to his mother and assisted her to the pillow at the other end of the table where she faced Julianne. We obediently spread our palms on the tablecloth.

Victor made one more preparation. Striking a wooden match, he lit a cone–shaped incense burner that sat atop a floor–model music box trimmed in silver. A snake of pungent smoke circled above us.

I waited for Alice to sneeze, but she sat frozen. Victor seated himself next to the music box and turned its little knob. Harp-like notes filled the room.

Madame Urina laid her hands before her on the table with her long, deep red fingernails spread out. In the candlelight, shadows swept from her long, mascara black eyelashes to her forehead. Eye-stinging incense smoke swirled before her. She moaned faintly in sync with the harp strings ringing from the music box and began to utter a sing-song chant.

"Spirits of the dead come into this room. Seek a soul." Madame Urina chanted so slowly that it was as if she was inventing one word at a time. "Seek and bring us one Lewiston Kelovich."

She repeated the chant over and over. It dragged on so long that I decided the moon must not be in the right place and the séance wasn't going to work after all.

Then an empty chair near the doorway moved. Wooden legs scraped the floor with a squeak that sent a shudder from my toes to my teeth. I held my breath. Julianne stayed motionless. Alice gasped again.

Victor raised a forefinger to his lips. "Shhhh."

Julianne laid her hand on mine as we stared at the chair that continued to wiggle by itself.

Madame Urina droned on."Speak to us, speak to us."

A pale stream of light poured though the room settling on the empty chair, or more exactly, on the zodiac drape just above the chair. An image appeared. It was an etched face bobbing unsteadily on the black fabric. It was the head of a man in a hat. The face was fuzzy, but I immediately thought of our photo of Lucky Lew standing over the bear.

Above the tinkling music box came a muffled male voice. "Look with favor on my former family. Give them good will with one another. Julianne, I beg you to do this for me."

Alice moaned and slumped over in a faint.

Instantly, the beam of light that had come from nowhere was gone. The image vanished with it. The music box stopped.

Both Julianne and I reached for Alice. With trembling hands I tugged on Alice's arm.

"Victor," Julianne snapped. "Please turn on the lights."

"Of course, and I'll fix Miss Allen up with

a glass of brandy."

Julianne and I rubbed Alice's hands and arms until she moaned feebly. Her eyes fluttered opened.

"That was scary!" I arose off my pillow on jittery legs.

"The séance was incredible, Mother. Isn't she marvelous, Julianne?" Victor beamed with a decanter in his hand. He poured brandy into a teacup.

Madame Urina did not wait for Julianne to reply. "I'm quite drained of energy. You must excuse me." As she swept from the room, I thought a faint line of amusement stretched across her red mouth.

Alice sat up on the sofa and gulped the brandy Victor offered. With a cough she said, "I would never have believed it if I hadn't seen it with my own eyes."

I was about to agree, but Julianne interrupted. "It's time we left." She pulled Alice to her feet. "It's getting dark and Slim will be wondering about us."

Julianne tossed me my coat from the wall peg. She hustled us out of the house so fast that coats were not buttoned and mittens weren't out of our pockets. Victor followed us to the car without taking time for a coat.

"These beasts are stubborn in cold weather. Please allow me to be of assistance." He reached into the cab for the throttle lever, brushing his arm across Julianne. "It'll need a little extra priming."

"Thanks for the séance, Victor" I said. "It was really...."

Julianne cut me off. "We appreciate your help in cranking the Ford, Victor."

He gave her a merry wink and retreated to the front of the car. The crank took several revolutions before the engine revved. His dark eyes were so sparkly that I thought he looked like someone who won a bet on a horse race. He called above the roaring motor, "I'll look forward to seeing you again, very soon."

"Thank your mother for an entertaining afternoon," Julianne said and throttled the Ford away in a skid over the snow-covered road.

"Entertaining afternoon? Don't you mean spooky, scary, creepy, terrifying?" Alice said.

"Believe me, both of you, it was all illusion. I don't know how they did it, but this is one time when you cannot believe your eyes."

"Julianne, I know what I saw. I'm sure Madame Urina has magical powers." My frustration came out in a shout. I didn't want that fantastic experience destroyed or watered down, not by anyone.

CHAPTER 23

Airplane Crash

When I told Slim the details of the séance, he roared with laughter. "Didn't I tell you that woman will stop at nothing to fool you? Now she's conjuring up the devil himself."

"It truly <u>was</u> magic. How else could a chair move all by itself?"

Slim wiped watery eyes on his sleeve. "I think I can conjure up that one. Watch this."

He rummaged in a kitchen drawer and took out a roll of twine. He tied a loop and told me to put it around the leg of a kitchen chair. With a trail of twine along the floor, he went into the pantry. He tugged on the twine, and Julianne came into the kitchen as the chair clattered to the floor.

We all laughed and Julianne said, "We get the idea. With a little practice and dim light, you, too, could perform the supernatural, Slim."

Thoughtfully, I picked up the chair. "I heard Victor mumbling when he was behind that curtain. It could be he was talking to someone who had hold of a string tied on the chair. Maybe someone like that Hector."

"You got it figured out." Slim rerolled the twine into a ball.

"That's not all that happened. We heard the ghost talk!"

Slim pulled on his long beard for a reflective moment. "I figure I know the answer to that one. Ever hear of a ventriloquist?"

With a fresh cup of coffee, Julianne settled at the table next to Slim. "Can Victor throw his voice?"

"I seen him at the Klondike Saloon with a dummy dressed up like a prospector."

I imagined Victor in his fancy vest with a funny, gold-panning doll on his lap. "You mean he can talk without moving his lips?"

"His lips might move some, but he can make his voice sound like it comes from any corner in a room."

I shook my head and thought hard about what we saw. "I didn't look at Victor's lips. It was Lucky Lew I was looking at."

"Yes." Julianne said. "A man's face appeared in a strange beam of light."

"I know it was him. At least, it sure looked like Lucky Lew does in that bear hunting photograph." I pulled the chair back up to the table.

"That one has me stumped. But, as sure as I know Jack Dempsey is the world boxing champ, I know they pulled it off with some trick."

"Gee whiz, how can I not believe what I saw? How can that be?" I moaned.

As the days passed, I continued to puzzle over the strange event. I wanted so much to tell Helen and Sissy, but dared not. Julianne, Alice and I had a pact not to let the story out. It was bad enough to have Slim laugh at us. If the whole town gossiped and laughed, how could we make anyone believe a murderer was on the loose?

At the end of the week, I was finishing my homework when Julianne came home from the airfield. She had news that thrilled me to the bone.

"Leif said he's doing the Nome flight tomorrow after taking mail to Ft. Yukon, then Galena. He wants me along to help with the mail and cargo tallies. He says there's plenty of room in the Fokker if you want to tag along, Tish."

I squealed with glee. I hadn't been in an airplane since school started.

"Both of you going off in a blasted flying machine?" Slim was in the doorway with a newspaper in his hand.

"Slim, it's the most fantastic airplane. It has fancy seats and drapes on the windows. It's just the spiffiest ever." I closed my book and we both followed Julianne into the kitchen.

Slim's cheeks turned red. "That blithering flyboy is likely to get you both killed."

"Rainbow has been flying up there nearly every week for three months now." Julianne pulled four skinned ptarmigan from the icebox. As Tilly had taught her, she dropped the birds into a pot of boiling water.

I began to spread my books and papers on the kitchen table. "The Fokker is a really safe airplane."

"No such thing as a safe flying machine. Besides, first you fly off to Ft. Yukon, then head the other way to Nome. Nome itself is over 600 miles from here. It's clear out to the Bering Sea."

Julianne called from the pantry, "That is all the more reason for Rainbow Flight Service to provide freight, passenger, and mail service."

"You know what's between here and there? There ain't nothing but mountains and rivers fixing to freeze up."

"We'll be making stops at Ft. Yukon and Galena," Julianne said.

I envisioned the big map on the airplane hangar wall. "Those villages are on the Yukon River."

"Leif says the landing fields at Ft. Yukon and Galena are good and the Nome field is wide open with no trees." Julianne put an onion on the cutting board.

I added more of my new knowledge. "Next summer the airfield here will get extended for more and bigger airplanes. Leif told me that."

All evening, as Slim went about his chores, he came up with new reasons why we should not fly off to Nome. When he stuffed kindling into the cook stove, he warned, "What about school? You're sure to miss at least one day."

"I'll turn in my homework on Tuesday."

He brought an armload of wood in for the hearth. "Smells like snow. A big storm might blow in."

"Leif won't fly if a storm comes up." I set out bowls for the ptarmigan stew.

When the bird and vegetables got cooked and smelled delectable, Julianne set the pot and a ladle in the middle of the table. "If a blizzard hits, we could be delayed a day or two, then you can expect us home on the first clear day."

By evening, when Slim had the furnace stoked with coal and came up from the basement, he was out of arguments. Although his grumbling continued then began again the next morning.

"I'm drivin' you to that dang airfield. I want to look that daredevil flyer in the eye."

The morning was clear and cold. I tied back the curtain on the kitchen window. "Look, Slim, there's not a cloud in the sky. It's a great day for flying."

A frown didn't leave his face even when I offered to turn the crank on the Ford. My first turn got nothing from under the hood. The second got a weak cough. I pulled hardest on the third try and the motor roared to life.

Julianne came out of the house carrying a

bag. We hopped aboard. With Slim behind the wheel, the tires bumped over clumps of snow at a speed slower than a waddling duck. It took twice as long to get to the field as would have if Julianne drove.

Slim limped the Ford onto the airfield and yanked on the handbrake. We stopped a few feet from the Fokker airplane. Its 240–horsepower engine idly purred.

Like an Olympic Games champ adorned in leather and neck scarf, Leif came trotting up to the Ford and opened the door. "The engine's all warmed up." He thrust his right hand out to Slim. "I'll have them back on Sunday, Slim."

With a frown, he grabbed hold of the hand thrust out to him. The handshake went words from Slim that I was glad I could not hear above the car and airplane engines chugging away.

Julianne and I took turns giving him a hug. We hustled aboard the airplane and continued to wave at him through windows when we settled into seats.

When Leif sat at the controls, the engine revved up. Skis on the Fokker rolled the length of the runway. I could see us headed straight for the Northern Commercial Company's stack of wood at the end of the field. With a last enormous push into the wind, we became airborne and made it over the top of the woodpile.

"We're in the air!" I shouted and let go of the handgrip. I pressed my nose against a window to see Slim standing with his good arm raised in a wave like a final farewell. We soared higher than Leif had ever taken me in the Jenny. My heart soared, too, as the sight of houses, cars, wagons, and dogsleds were quickly reduced to miniature toys. Slim, too, quickly became a speck that faded from sight.

Julianne let go of her handgrip too and gazed down at the rapidly changing landscape. From the cockpit, Leif glanced back at us and gave a thumbs-up sign. Noise from the hard-working engine and giant propeller drowned out any possible conversation.

Unlike the smaller airplanes, this Fokker had us in an enclosed cab that was warm and comfortable. It smelled of new leather. Being as plush as a Pullman car on a train, it had four upholstered passenger seats and matching red velvet curtains. Two of the seats were piled with wooden boxes containing fresh eggs, fruit and vegetables. It was cargo for merchants and needed to be protected from freezing.

Inside the cab with a roof, we were not in danger of falling out when the plane tipped one way or the other. If the plane should hit air currents, passengers had hand stirrups to hang onto. But this was not a rough ride. Julianne and I could move about. She opened a picnic basket and passed around peanut butter sandwiches.

In a short while, all we could see below was snow-covered wilderness so I turned away from the window. My heart was singing so I motioned for Julianne to sing with me. We sang, *Daisy, Daisy, give me your answer do.*

Leif joined in too. We laughed and sang our way through song after song. Icy rivers, frosted valleys and foreboding mountains passed beneath us. Somewhere in the middle of *Take Me Out to the Ball Game*, I noticed Leif had stopped singing. He was totally fixed on flying the plane.

Below and ahead of us, I spotted a vast river that was a mixture of floating ice and open water. I crouched behind the pilot's seat. "Is that the Yukon River?"

He was so absorbed in the control panel that he did not answer. When he did look at me, his eyes were dead serious.

"What's the matter? Are we lost?" I shouted with a grin.

Leif shook his head. "It's the gas. We're out. I have to set her down. Now!"

Julianne spun forward. "How can it be out

of gasoline? We watched Jess fill up the tank yesterday?"

"Maybe we can make it to Circle," he yelled.

"Maybe?" Julianne screeched and pulled me back to our seats. We peered anxiously from the window for a sign of a village.

"We're going down, aren't we, Julianne?" We clung to each other.

"Button up your coat. Put on your mittens. Hold on tight. Leif will find a good spot on the riverbank." Julianne's voice held no conviction.

Leif was flying us away from the ice-infested river. The nose pointed down to a snowy forest. White ground rushed up to us.

"Hang on!" he shouted.

A wing clipped a tree and pieces of spruce scraped the windows. In seconds, the plane banged down in a clearing. Its skis skidded on and on and tilted up an incline. Julianne and I tumbled to the floor.

The airplane plunged into a snowdrift. Its nose went down and the tail rose up. My fingers clutched a hand–stirrup. The seat fell away leaving my whole body dangling in the air. I squealed as the airplane did a somersault.

CHAPTER 24

The Hot Springs

"We're upside down!" I lay sprawled on the ceiling, looking up at the floor. Seats bolted to the floor dangled down at me. My lap was full of oranges. I struggled to push aside a busted box to see Julianne. She was entangled in a window curtain and pinned against a crate. "Are you alive, Julianne?"

"I... think... so."

"Julianne, Tish!" Leif's voice rang with fear. He was out of the plane and the whole thing jolted as he popped the cabin door open. "Are you hurt?"

I crawled toward him. "I'm good."

Leif's strong hands reached in and lifted me to the ground. He crawled into the plane and gently pulled Julianne out onto the snow. She leaned against him with a mitten held to her forehead. "Where are we?"

"We're in a softball field at Arctic Circle Hot Springs. Are you sure you're not injured?" Leif looked us over as if he was counting legs and arms.

I rubbed a tender spot on my shoulder. "I'm kind of bruised."

"A softball field?" Julianne said in a dazed way.

"Yes. It wasn't long enough for a smooth landing, but I expect help to show up here any minute." Leif went on to explain that we were in the heart of gold-mining country. Miners were scattered in the hills and across the valley. "Anyone nearby who heard or saw the plane will come."

"Wow, look at the Fokker." I stared aghast at the beautiful, proud body lying belly up like a dead horse.

"It'll take work, but the snow saved it from being a total loss." Leif kept a firm grip on Julianne as if concerned about her balance.

Barking rang out from the forest. "There's a dogsled coming." I said, spotting a team of dogs trotting out from behind frosty trees and into the clearing.

"Are people coming?" Julianne mumbled in an uncertain way.

"You better sit down." Leif settled her on a snow bank. He hastily pulled a blanket out of the cab of the plane and tucked it in around her.

Amid a chorus of barks, whines and howls, dogs pulled up and the sled came to a stop. The musher was a man with a red bushy beard, thick eyebrows and a broad smile. "Hey, Bjorgam, what kind of a stunt was that?"

"Good to see you, Buck." Leif vigorously shook the man's hand. "Just thought I'd prove the Fokker doesn't really need a 900-foot runway."

"Only if you want to land right side up," Buck retorted.

The men laughed and all nine dogs chimed in with more barks and wagging tails. I knelt to pet the handsome malamute lead dog.

"Good to see your passengers survived." Buck's big gloved hand touched the top of my knit hat.

I started to speak but stopped at hearing the voices of other men approaching. Three men came hiking over a ridge. They greeted Leif in joking ways but quickly worked with him to lift the airplane's tail and set the Fokker upright.

As everyone examined the damage, they

gave opinions about how to fix the wreck. I stuck close to Leif's side and listened to every word. I was glad to hear they agreed the twisted propeller might be straightened. All decided the damaged tubing on the rudder could be repaired.

I caught a strong scent in the cold air. "Leif, I smell gasoline."

"Right, Tish, it looks like there's a puncture in the gas tank." He shook his head with disbelief.

An Athabascan man named Pete pointed to a discolored spot. "It looks like that tank was stabbed with something as sharp as the blade of a pocket knife."

"I swear that tank had no hole when it was filled," Leif said.

"Something like that would have to be intentional," Buck said.

Pete ran bare fingers over the damaged metal. "It sure looks like a gummy tar was smeared all around this hole."

Buck took off a glove and touched the hole with a bare finger. "Tar could hold for a while, so if a culprit is at fault, no one would be the wiser before you got off the ground."

"Why would someone ever want to do

that to the Fokker?" I asked and stared from one man to the next. Each new face encircled by fur-trimmed hoods wore the lines of hard-earned wisdom, yet each looked puzzled.

Pete looked at me as if he hadn't noticed me before. "Some folks like the old ways best." Weathered lines in his face left no doubt that his knowledge of old ways stretched far back into his Indian heritage.

"Airplanes pose a threat to freighters who are dog mushers or steam boat operators," Leif added.

Buck snorted. "Hits them right in the wallet."

Leif threw up his hands. "Yet, I can't think of one man who would get violent about it."

They all began to mention names and talk at length about people I didn't know. I wandered back to Julianne who got unsteadily to her feet. I told her about how the gas tank probably got stabbed with a knife. "No one can guess who would have done such a thing."

Julianne looked at me in a dazed way. "I know it was because of me. I was the target again."

Cold suddenly seeped through my coat and boots. I reached for my sister's hand. "How can that be true? No one but Slim knew we would be on board the plane."

"You ask about the truth?" Her eyes blinked and blinked again. "Too much evil has happened."

She dropped my hand and touched a mitten to her cheek. "On the ship, Hector's beard scraped my cheek, and he was a drunk shouting at us on the bridge. Constable Dole ignored us. There was deceit in Victor's antics, and Stella tried to dupe us with a magical hoax. Lucky Lew lay there pleading with eyes that were tired and spotted with blood, and then...." Julianne's voice drifted away. She crumpled onto the snow.

"Julianne!"

Leif was instantly there. He held Julianne. With his glove pulled off, he stroked her brow with a bare hand and cuddled her with hugging arms.

I rubbed one of her hands, mitten and all. I called her name over and over, desperately willing her eyes to open. Slowly, they did. "Julianne, you fainted." A hint of panic squeezed the sound of my voice.

"I'm fine. I was dizzy for a minute, but I'm fine now."

Leif shook his head. "You're not exactly

fine."

Buck said, "Young lady, you're going to the lodge for hot coffee and a soft bed. You've had a shock and that's nothing to shrug off."

"Julianne, this is Buck Murphy. He'll take you to the lodge." Leif picked her up in his arms. "Tish will go with you."

"You come too. Please, Leif," I pleaded like a little kid.

"I'll be along when damaged parts are off the plane." Leif set Julianne gently down on the sled. "I'll be able to work on them in Buck's garage."

"We will be fine," Julianne said weakly.

"With a good rest you will be. Tish, the same for you too."

Leif had me snuggle against Julianne. When he had us under wolf skins that were on the sled, he motioned Buck to take off.

Behind nine tails proudly held high, we bounced over a packed trail. Under a pale blue sky, the sun sparkled on a snowy meadow. Birch trees bordered the valley. Low hills were covered in thick spruce forests while mountain peaks stood treeless.

"Gee," Buck called, and the dog team turned abruptly onto a different trail. After a few minutes, buildings came into view. "That's the hotel, and over there is the general store."

A two-story building loomed in the clear blue sky. Steam rose in puffs of fog from a hot water spring. Buck pointed out a greenhouse where summer vegetables grew, a sprinkle of log cabins and a steaming swimming pool. The air was pungent with the smell of sulfur given off by the natural hot water.

"Whoa," Buck stomped on the sled brake. All the dogs yipped and barked at the front steps of the hotel. A woman, barely taller than me, came out of the door. She wore an apron over a wool skirt and sweater, but no coat. Her hands were planted firmly on her hips. "So this is what that wild flyer brought in."

"Bjorgam's airplane crashed with these ladies aboard." Buck helped Julianne out of the sled. "This is my wife, Gradelle Murphy."

I jumped up from the sled and hurried up the steps where the little woman grasped my hands in hers. "It's a wonder you're alive."

Julianne came up the steps and announced, "I'm Julianne Dushan, er... Kelovich, and this is my sister Matisha."

Buck let out an ear-piercing whistle. "Get, you huskies." He waved at us as the dogs headed back down the trail.

"Come inside. I have hot cocoa and a fresh pot of coffee," said the lady with a friendly smile. Laugh lines edged the corners of her light brown eyes.

"Cocoa is what I need." My teeth chattered with cold.

In the lobby we stepped on a braided rug of many colors. It lay on the hardwood floor. A massive rock fireplace crackled with burning birch logs. Green plants grew in pots on the windowsills. Gold-colored drapes hung at the windows, and a big fan spun from overhead log beams. White lace doilies lay on the tops of end tables and on the backs of lounge chairs.

"This lobby rivals a Seattle hotel. It's lovely," Julianne said. "I'm sure this is an oasis in the wilderness for gold miners."

"You've got that right," Mrs. Murphy said.

"I've never been to a real hot springs, not in my whole life," I said. Outside the window was a fascinating scene. I could see steam rising into the air.

"After having ginger cookies, you might want to go for a warm swim," she said.

"Oh yes, let's, Julianne."

My sister walked into the dining hall as if she didn't have the energy to answer me. There

257

were a dozen tables with bench-style seats. All were empty undoubtedly because it was in the middle of the afternoon.

Gradelle pointed to the table closest to the kitchen. With agile movement, she brought a steaming mug of coffee to Julianne and hot cocoa to me. As I inhaled the creamy smell, every jitter and shiver in my body dissolved.

A plate piled high with cookies appeared before us and Gradelle sat down across from us. "I heard all about the way you two came up here from the Lower 48 so you could marry with Lucky Lew."

"True," Julianne said. I blew in my mug to cool it and thought how strange it was to hear people say "Lower 48" when talking about the States.

"It was a pity what happened to a good man like that," Gradelle said. "Pneumonia, wasn't it?"

"He was in a car crash," I said with a bite of a delicious ginger-oatmeal cookie.

Julianne nodded. "His injuries led to pneumonia. Did you know him well?"

My sister didn't sound like her real self. Her voice was kind of impersonal. She could have been talking about President William Harding dying from pneumonia as he returned from his visit to Alaska. Lucky Lew and President Harding were hardly the same. Julianne's face was pale.

"He came here to the lodge frequently." Gradelle stirred a spoon of sugar into a mug of steaming coffee. "He loved to soak in the hot pools, especially after moose hunting in the fall."

I began to rub my arm and shoulder. "I can hardly wait to get into the pool. My shoulder is sore from banging around in the plane crash."

"You poor little lamb." Gradelle laid a hand on my shoulder then looked at Julianne with concern in her eyes. "A warm soaking will be a good cure for you too, Julianne."

"I'm afraid we have no swimsuits." She listlessly sipped coffee.

"Francine," Gradelle hollered across the dining hall to a woman who came in a side door. She carried a large clothesbasket filled with laundry off rows of clotheslines in the yard. "I want to see if we have swimsuits in there that will fit these two gals."

The strong-built woman wore pants like a man. She cheerfully carried the laundry basket to the table. She pulled towels from it and carried an armload away, leaving the basket.

Gradelle said, "I can't promise a pretty one. These are swimsuits we keep on hand for visitors around here."

"I'll pick out swimsuits for both me and my sister." I eagerly dug through the laundry that felt icy. Everything was dry but stiff from freezing on clotheslines.

Julianne cupped unsteady hands around her mug. "Alright, Tish, let's do try the pool for a few minutes."

As I shook out one mysterious garment after another, I followed an urge and asked, "Mrs. Murphy, did you ever meet our father?"

Julianne said, "He was Jonah Dushan, everyone called him Jonsey. He and Lew had mined together years ago."

"Can't say as I ever met the man. But there's someone staying here who worked with Lucky Lew for years. Tim Riley would be the one to ask."

Instantly, Julianne's eyes lost the glaze from her fainting spell. "As a matter of fact, Timothy Riley is someone we've been anxious to meet."

"He is always around at dinner time." Gradelle rummaged through the laundry basket. She pulled out something with orange stripes. "This is my smallest one, Tish."

I held it up to my shoulders and decided it would fit. I dug into the basket again and pulled out a blue, baggy one for Julianne. "These two will be okay."

Julianne had no opinion. Her thoughts were apparently on Tim Riley.

Gradelle gathered up the cups. "Good. I need to get the evening meal started. Your room is right up the stairs, number five."

We thanked her and I hurried up the stairs taking two at a time. At the top, I paused for Julianne to catch up and peeked into the bathroom marked *Ladies*. There was a shower, a long mirror, and a pull-chain commode. We passed numbered doors down the hall. Number five was cozy and warm with hot water flowing through a coiled radiator.

"Those feather pillows look tempting," Julianne said.

"A swim first. You promised." I pushed the blue swimsuit into her hands.

We undressed and pulled on the swimsuits. The styles were hopelessly out of date, and we laughed at each other. Wearing boots and coats, we carried towels down the stairs and through the lobby.

The pool was outside the hotel and down a path banked by snow. The cold air covered the water in thick steam. In the fog, I could see no other bathers. As fast as I could shed my coat and boots, I jumped in and came up with my bobbed hair plastered wet against my head.

"It's warm, Julianne. Jump in."

Julianne shivered in the frigid air but quickly slipped into the pool.

The water was very warm and felt luxurious. It had a soothing effect on both of us, but it wasn't long before Julianne said it had sapped her energy. My legs and arms felt heavy, too. When I dragged my hot body out, the cold air surprisingly did not sting.

We retreated to our room, dried off and snuggled into the feather bed. We both fell asleep within seconds and napped until a loud knock startled us awake.

CHAPTER 25

Dogsled Solution

"Hey, you two, don't sleep through dinner," Leif called through the door. Julianne jumped up and wrapped herself in a quilt. She opened the door and Leif poked his head in. He grinned at a rumpled Julianne.

"Not a chance, I'm ravenous."

"I'm starving too." With a yawn I snuggled up to my pillow.

"I thought you could use this." Leif handed in our carpetbag. "Hope you packed a hair brush."

"Go away!" Julianne grabbed the bag and pushed the door shut. Through the door, we heard him chuckle as boots clomped down the hall.

"I'm glad he brought me some socks." I

woke up a little more. "Do you think Leif got the plane fixed?"

Julianne groped through the bag. "From his expression, I'd say definitely not."

"Good, I love it here. I hope we can stay for a week."

"That long will make Slim worry out of his wits. He will have no idea where we are." Julianne tossed socks to me and began brushing tangles from her damp hair.

"Poor Slim. What can we do about that?"

"At least for the moment, there's no way he knows we've crashed."

Boisterous male voices came from the dining hall. Our entrance caused a stir. Only men were seated at the tables and they exercised good manners by standing up in the presence of ladies. Nearly everyone removed his hat. I did as Julianne and nodded until the men sat down again. Conversations resumed but none in loud voices. I guessed the story of Lucky Lew's widow was spreading.

All eyes followed us as we crossed the room to where Leif was waiting. I scooted onto the bench next to him. Julianne sat across the table. Gradelle bustled about loading tables with platters of succulent salmon, bowls of mashed potatoes, milk gravy, steamed carrots and peas, and sourdough bread. She called, "There's blueberry pie for dessert."

As serving dishes were passed, we asked Leif questions about the airplane. He talked about why the repairs might take most of a week. By dessert time, Buck, who had been kept busy helping in the kitchen, joined us. Julianne asked him if Timothy Riley was in the room.

"Hey Tim," Buck called to a man bent over his plate. "Come here and meet these people."

A man with stubby whiskers on a deeply lined face shook his head.

"Yeah, come on. They don't bite."

Riley glanced around at other diners who stared his way. Slowly he got to his feet. His puffy eyes scanned the room like those of a wild animal checking for open doors and possible escape. As he approached us, he rubbed the palms of his hands on his overalls as if to wipe off dirt.

Buck took Riley by the arm and introduced us all. With hesitation he accepted Leif's handshake. He yanked off his hat and gave a quick nod to Julianne, then to me.

I couldn't resist saying, "Oh, Mr. Riley, you're Lucky Lew's friend that he left money to."

"Friend?" Riley scowled at me. He slumped onto the seat next to Buck. "Well, I worked for the man."

"The attorney has been trying to locate you. Have you heard from Steven Mills?" Julianne asked.

His thin eyebrows went up, sending a ripple of lines across a wide forehead that receded to sparse hair. His wary eyes narrowed. "What's he want?"

Julianne leaned across the table and spoke in a hushed tone. "In his will, Lew Kelovich bequeathed twelve thousand dollars to you."

Riley's red-blotched eyes blinked again and again. His sunburned face turned crimson. The table rocked as he sprang to his feet. "What'd he do that for?"

"You must've been a good foreman, Tim," Buck said. He stood up and slapped Riley heartily on his back. "Congratulations."

"What'd he do that for?" Riley repeated and turned away. He stalked out of the dining room grumbling and panting as if he had run up a mountain.

I cupped my hands to my mouth and

whispered to Julianne, "I don't like that man."

Leif heard my not-so-quiet whisper and chuckled. He said, "Riley looks like a man who's been guzzling too much hooch."

"You got that right," Buck said. "Riley has worked out at the Grayson gold claim since midsummer. That's where they mine a little gold and brew a lot of white lightening. They got a big still out there."

"But making whiskey isn't legal." I said as I reached for a slice of wild blueberry pie.

"Prohibition may be on, but no U.S. marshal has been this way since Leif flew one in last August."

"I remember that well. When I picked him up a week later, he said no one would tell him where the bootleggers were. He was one disappointed lawman."

Everyone laughed except Julianne who looked distracted. "Leif, do you really think we will be able to fly out of here in a few days?"

"We can patch the gas tank and straighten the rudder tubing with no problem, but I don't like the looks of that hairline crack in the propeller."

"Well, let's go down to the garage and take another look at it," Buck said.

I spooned down the last of my tasty pie. "May we come too?"

"Glad for the company," Leif said with eyes lingering on Julianne.

Julianne walked from the dining room with us, but she didn't seem to be listening. I guessed her thoughts were still on strange old Tim Riley.

In the lobby, Leif asked, "Coming, Julianne?"

Julianne's gaze met his. She smiled and took his hand. I grabbed her other hand. We followed Buck out of the hotel and down a path to the garage.

After tinkering and puttering in the garage, Leif reached a conclusion. "It's too risky. We need a replacement for that prop."

"Somebody's bound to be hitting the trail for Fairbanks before long," Buck said.

"When we get word to Jess, the boss will fly a replacement out in the Jenny." Leif sighed heavily. "Until then, we might as well enjoy the hot springs."

I clapped happily. "Let's go night swimming."

Leif's arm was around Julianne's waist and he held my hand as we stepped out of the garage. The frosted night sky was filled with dancing northern lights. "How utterly beautiful," Julianne sighed.

"There are streaks of red and green in the aurora borealis." I showed off my new classroom knowledge.

"Listen real careful and sometimes you'll hear them crackle," Buck said.

I listened hard, but heard only a loud cackle. A jolly laugh came from the direction of the hotel.

"Hey Buck," called a man I'd seen in the dining hall. "This is my lucky night. I just sold a sled and dogs for twice what they're worth. That Riley is throwing cash around like a rich man."

"Yeah? I've never figured him for a dog musher." Buck walked ahead of us but we could hear every word in the quiet night.

"No, he don't even like dogs. But he has a big hankering to get to Fairbanks as fast as he can," the man said.

"Sounds like just the man I need to see," Leif said. In the hotel lobby, Tim Riley agreed to take a message to Jess Younker.

"I'll head out at first light tomorrow. Should get there in two days if the weather holds."

Abruptly, Julianne said, "I'd like to go with you, Mr. Riley. I need to get back to town."

Leif looked startled, and I sure was.

"Yeah, if you come along, I don't have to bother with no message about that flying machine. But it won't be no Sunday buggy ride." He walked away with Buck to buy dog food and supplies.

"Please don't go, Julianne," I pleaded. "Why don't you want to stay here with us?"

"If Riley were to deliver the news of the crash, Slim will be terribly frightened." Julianne put her hands on my shoulders. "Besides, I have a very strong feeling Tim Riley can shed light on Lew's death."

"I don't think that cranky man will tell you anything."

"I think Tish has a point there," Leif said. "My advice is not to go charging off on a 125-mile wild goose chase."

"Riley is difficult, but this will give me time and opportunity to pry information from him."

The determined look Leif received let him know he couldn't change Julianne's mind. He shrugged. The man my sister had called arrogant and confident looked helpless. I felt sorry for him and totally irritated at my sister. I pulled away from her. "Let's go swimming, Leif."

"That sounds pretty good, Tish."

"I'm going to see about food for the trip and get packed," Julianne said.

"I have a beaver parka with a wolf ruff for you to take. You'll need it."

"Thank you, Leif." The cheerful way she said it made me think she was thanking him for not calling her foolish or just plain stupid. That's what I'd expect most men to say. Yet, I wished he would say those things if it could keep her from going off on a dogsled.

"I'll get the coat to you in the morning before you take off." Leif watched her walk away.

I headed for the stairs and my swimsuit. "Come on, Leif. Let's go jump in the hot water."

Leif and I soaked in the pool for a while without laughing or talking much. Then Leif climbed out and told me he was going to work on the airplane some more.

I dragged myself back to the room dripping water into my boots from the soggy swimsuit. I found Julianne taking a heavy sweater from our bag.

"I want to go with you, Julianne."

"I'm leaving this bag for you." She threw a towel over my hair and rubbed my head vigorously. "There will be no room for you. With all of Riley's gear and me on the sled, those dogs have all they can handle."

"Fiddlesticks. I don't want you to go away. It scares me."

"Get out of that wet suit, Tish." She handed me another towel. "Leif will take good care of you."

"You really like him, don't you, Julianne?"

"Of course."

"You know what I mean, not like just any friend. I can tell he thinks you're special."

"You can?" She held my chin and looked at me with smiling eyes. "You're still trying to marry me off, aren't you?"

"No, not anymore."

"How come?" She tossed my nightgown, letting it fall over my head.

"Because we are a family, you and me and Slim. Lucky Lew cheated Papa. I was wrong to want you to marry him."

"You couldn't have known."

"But I would never want you to be married to a man like that. I was only thinking of myself and what I wanted."

Julianne planted a kiss on my forehead. "I think my little sister is growing up."

We said our night prayers together, the way we did when mother was alive. Peaceful sleep came in minutes.

As soon as Julianne stirred in the pre-dawn dark, I jumped up and pulled on my long wool stockings, boots, and wrinkled dress. I led the way down the stairs to the lobby where a single kerosene lamp burned dimly. Leif was there, slumped in an armchair. His eyes were closed, head resting on a shaggy fur coat.

Julianne smiled and whispered, "With that look of little-boy innocence, can this be the same flamboyant flyer who strode into that cafe in Seward?"

"Hey, Leif." I nudged his shoulder and giggled at the way his eyes popped open.

"Did you sleep all night in that chair?" Julianne asked.

"I didn't want to miss you." He sleepily staggered to his feet.

Dogs barked outside and I rushed to the

window. "Tim Riley is putting the dogs in harnesses."

Leif wrapped a heavy fur coat around Julianne, holding onto it as he looked into her face. "Be careful when you get back to town. It was no accident that the plane went down."

"I'm sure it happened because of me."

"Why? Who would do that?" I moaned. A chill shivered through me.

"It's not likely that damage to the plane had anything to do with you." Leif's gaze held her as if he was seeing more than the lovely face of a friend. His mouth opened but he choked back words as if he didn't trust what he might say. Instead, he dropped his grip on the fur coat. "I know the answer is in Fairbanks. Promise you'll be careful." He turned toward barking dogs and went out the front door.

I pressed against the window and watched him help harness eleven huskies. The excited dogs yelped, wiggled and breathed white puffs into the cold air. When it looked like the dogs were ready, we went out.

Julianne hurriedly settled into the sled. Leif barely got fur robes tucked around her when Riley whistled and stepped off the brake. The sled lunged forward.

I waved until I could no longer see the

trotting dogs pull the sled. They disappeared into the frosted forest, bound toward icy rivers, rolling hills and windswept mountains.

CHAPTER 26

Evidence Discovered

Leif and I walked back into the lodge. Gradelle Murphy called to us, "Come have some cocoa, little gal. You too, Leif."

We sipped the warm drink and ate toast with wild raspberry jam. Gradelle entertained us with stories. She told us about long trips she had made by dogsled and snowshoes. With her finger on the table she traced the trail from the hot springs to Fairbanks.

"I told Julianne to make sure Tim Riley stops for the night at Miller House. It's the one place on the trail where you can get a bunk and a warm meal."

"They should get to town in about a day and a half." Leif sounded calm, but his brow was wrinkled in a deep frown.

"Now don't you be worrying about that spunky gal. She has the spirit it takes to make that trip. You got a plane to fix and Tish can swim all she wants."

Both Leif and I followed her advice. Luckily the orange–striped swimsuit had dried out by the radiator. I put it on and swam in the fog–covered pool until my hands and feet were full of puffy wrinkles. After emerging from hot water onto the snowy path to the lodge, I felt restless. I got myself dressed and was glad Gradelle let me help in the kitchen before and after lunch.

Francine let me help her, too. I put fresh towels in the rooms and gathered up magazines and papers that renters left behind. The room vacated by Tim Riley was really messy. Before Francine came in pushing her broom, I found a whole newspaper under the bed.

It was a copy of the *Daily News-Miner* dated in June. I had seen that edition, but this time horror crept over me. The story of his death and a photograph of Lucky Lew were on the front page. An 'X' was splashed across Lucky Lew's face. There were swearwords scribbled over the story. The margins were filled with bad scribbles that read, "The bastard deserved it! He had to die for my boy! Now, Donnie will rest in peace."

I gasped, "Julianne's with the killer!"

Clutching the newspaper, I ran from the room through the hotel and down the path to Buck's garage. I burst through the door.

"Tish, where's your coat?" Buck wiped his greasy hands on a rag. "T'aint summer, you know."

"Is Leif here? I need to see him right now."

"He hiked down to the airplane. The hole in the tank is patched and we got the rudder tube straight. It should work just fine."

"I must see him."

"He'll be along soon. It's coming up on supper time."

"I can't wait. It's Julianne. She's in terrible danger." My breathless words spilled out.

"Now, now, sweetie, don't you be fretting. Your sister's going to be just fine. They got good dogs and the weather is clear."

"You don't understand. She really is in danger." I puckered up and tried to hold back tears.

"Okay, sweetheart, you run and get a jacket. I'll hook up a few dogs and we'll get to the plane in no time." Buck patted my back, acting as if he was afraid I'd get hysterical.

On the trail, I poured out the whole story to Buck about the cut cable that caused Lucky Lew's car to roll into the canyon. Standing behind me on the runners of the sled, he listened patiently. I'm not sure he believed me before we reached Leif and the airplane.

I hopped out of the sled and quickly spread out the newspaper on a wing. "Look Leif, this is proof that Tim Riley did it. He killed Lucky Lew."

Both Leif and Buck read the scribbled messages. Frowns turned into alarm on the two stunned faces.

"Looks like Riley has a screw or two loose," Buck said.

Color drained from Leif's face. "Julianne's with him."

"What can we do, Leif?" I pulled on his sleeve.

"Fly to Fairbanks as fast as possible. Let's patch that propeller as best we can, Buck, then get the gas tank filled. I'm taking off in the morning as soon as it's light."

"You mean <u>we</u>. I'm coming with you." My voice shivered.

Leif and Buck looked at one another. Leif nodded.

Repairing the airplane became our obsession. I helped in the passenger compartment by scraping frozen eggshells off the walls and pushing boxes out of the middle of the floor. I picked up scattered blankets, a curtain and magazines. Leif and Buck worked to install the rudder. When it was finally in place, we returned to the garage to work on the propeller.

Leif and Buck hammered and reshaped metal in an ear-crushing clang of steel. Gradelle and I brought them steaming bowls of moose stew for dinner. Butterflies in my stomach and the smell of motor oil and grease took my appetite away. I ended the evening in the lodge helping Gradelle wash up dishes.

The night proved long and almost sleepless. My thoughts were overwhelmed with scary visions of Julianne with the killer. In dreams I kept remembering Slim say, "Idiot will get you both killed."

The temperature dropped in the night, and the next morning it was so bitterly cold that we could not take off at dawn after all. To keep the engine from freezing solid, Leif and Buck formed a tent out of blankets and covered the nose. They left burning lanterns in that tent to warm the engine. It was nearly noon when we finally climbed aboard.

We were out on the field alone. The

extreme cold kept everyone else away. Even Buck said he'd be watching from the lodge with his fingers crossed.

"Will the plane fly when it's thirty-five below zero?" I asked through chattering teeth.

"It's got to." Leif tried for a fourth time to get the engine to turn over. His jaw was clenched. Tension dug hard lines in his face. On the fifth try, the engine coughed then sputtered to life, but still Leif resisted pressing it into action.

After a few minutes, my patience ran out. "Let's go, Leif. We've got to hurry."

"A little longer, until the engine warms up. We can't have it stall out when we're airborne."

I nodded, knowing he would not take an unnecessary chance. Even now, with little sleep and lots of worry, his hands were calm on the controls. I knew if anyone could get the airplane off the ground, it would be Leif.

Inside my mittens, I kept my icy fingers crossed.

Leif gunned the engine to break the skis loose from snow. The plane taxied down the bumpy, frozen meadow. We slid to within inches of bordering trees. Leif turned the plane to have a runway as long as was possible. The engine roared louder. I held on and squeezed my eyes shut as the skis beneath us bumped and bounced, gathering ground speed. Then the bumping vanished. We were airborne.

A thud made my eyes pop open. We were low and rocked from side to side. The dangling skis had brushed treetops, and spruce boughs floated in our wake. We were climbing. The engine roared loud, and it was steady, as it took us higher and higher.

I slapped Leif on the shoulder and he flashed me a grin. "I knew you could do it," I shouted.

The sky was sunny bright and the air was clear. As we leveled off, the engine noise toned down to a mellow, even beat. Warmth from the engine filled the cab, but a thawing body did not soothe turbulent thoughts. Julianne was all I could think about.

The time in the air seemed endless. Finally though, Fairbanks appeared below us and Leif landed the plane without a hitch. When he switched off the engine, I was astonished at the scene before us.

"What's going on?"

"Beats me," Leif said.

Nearly every dog team, horse-drawn wagon and automobile in town converged on the airfield despite the cold temperature. This town that had learned to take the coming and going of aircraft in stride, put focused attention on the landing of the Fokker.

Jess, trailed by Alice Allen, came running across the field. As soon as my feet hit the ground, Alice threw her arms around me.

"You're safe! You're alive! Oh, Tish, you're here." She sobbed and wiped tears on frosty mittens.

"I'm okay, Alice. Why were you so worried? We weren't even due back until tomorrow?" Bewildered, I let her hug me.

Jess pounded joyfully on Leif's back and through steaming breath, his raspy voice said, "Thanks to that crazy Malone, half the town is worried."

"Which Malone?" I asked, thinking how all three, mother and sons, seemed a little crazy.

"Hector. His brother, Victor, got Constable Dole to lock him up for murder. Seems Hector got roaring drunk and told Victor the airplane wouldn't be flying back after what he did to it."

"So, that bum is finally locked up," Leif said.

Jess nodded. "They say Victor sobbed

crocodile tears over little Tish and Julianne being on a doomed airplane."

"Where's Julianne?" Alice stretched up to the airplane door.

"Didn't she ride in by dog team?" Leif asked. "She and Riley should have been here by noon."

"Tim Riley? No one's seen him for months," Jess said.

"Oh, oh, Leif." Our eyes met in mutual distress.

"Why wouldn't Julianne be on the airplane instead of a dogsled?" Alice was astonished.

"Jess, is the Jenny fueled up?"

"The tank's full, skis on, and warmed up. The boss was fixing to go search for you."

"I need to take it up. Julianne is in real danger."

"Danger?" Alice squeezed her arms around me. "What kind of danger?"

I patted her arms squeezing me. "We know it was Tim Riley who cut the brake cable on the Bearcat. Now, Julianne is with him on a dogsled. They're on the way to town."

Leif glanced at me with determination in his eyes, "Let's go." He started toward the Jenny, calling back to Jess, "Contact Constable Dole. Let him know Riley needs to be arrested."

I spotted Slim striding briskly across the field. The wolf ruff on his hooded parka made his face barely visible. As I ran after Leif, I shouted in frosty puffs, "Alice, please tell Slim we'll be back real soon."

CHAPTER 27

Dark Gold Mine

In the open cockpit of the Jenny, Leif and I were bundled up in blankets and scarves with everything covered except our eyes. Leif flew low and I trained my goggles on the ground. Through the river delta and gold dredge country, there were no signs of Tim Riley and the dogsled. We climbed into the hills.

At the treeless summit, I spotted something move. My shout, muffled in wool, rose above the Jenny's engine, "Down there. It's a dog team!"

"That's the Cleary Mine. Hang on, we're landing."

"Landing where? There's no place to land." My stare riveted on snow-covered brush and rocks below.

The Jenny swooped in an arc. Under the late afternoon sun, the snow was striped with shadows. The plane glided onto a narrow furrow where the summer road lay buried. Skis under the fuselage slipped along the steep uphill grade. The plane slid up the crest of the mountain until nothingness loomed beyond the propeller.

I screeched. The plane shuddered and came to a stop. The nose rested on the tip of the summit ridge, inches from slipping down the slope.

"You did it," I uttered without breathing and tossed off my goggles.

Leif grinned at me. "Yeah, I'm surprised too. Come on, let's get to the mine."

A chinook wind was sweeping across the mountains, and the air warmed to almost above freezing. I was astounded at how warm it felt. The mine was a short hike from the airplane. Leif easily jogged with his long legs over the icy hard-packed snow. I ran, slipped, slid, and didn't keep up. Perspiration built up under my coat.

Dogs barked in the wind and became frantic when they spotted Leif. As I caught up, the dogs pulled against the tie-down and twisted wildly in their harnesses.

From a half-way point on the ridge, I saw a sign over the entrance to a cave in the hillside read, *Cleary Summit Mine.* Tim Riley appeared at the cave entrance. A silver whiskey flask was raised in his hand. He hollered, "Shut up you mutts!"

I cupped my hands to my mouth and yelled, "Where's my sister?"

Riley's head snapped our way. He staggered to the dogsled, untied the rope stretched from the lead dog to a tree. Apparently, he did not recall the back of the sled was securely tied to a hitching post. He stepped onto the runners and yelled, "Yaw! Gee, Gee!"

The dogs lunged forward making the restraining rope taut. The sled tipped one way then the other.

"Whoa!" Leif yelled. The lead dog hesitated at conflicting commands. He grabbed the lead dog's collar.

At that moment a loose dog appeared from behind thick brush. It dashed past Leif and lunged at Riley, knocking the man off the sled. Riley sprawled on the snow with the dog snarling inches from his face.

"Get him off me." Riley hid his face from sharp teeth.

"Stay!" Leif commanded. The dog backed away but continued to snarl. Leif grabbed Riley by the throat of his jacket and pulled him to his feet.

Riley wiped a bare, bloody hand on his coat. "I should have kicked that dog to death when I had the chance."

I ran up to him and breathlessly shouted, "What have you done with Julianne?"

"Your sister's dead by now. You're too late."

Leif let fly a blow to Riley's jaw, knocking him into a snow bank. "Where is she?"

"Down there." Riley tilted his head toward the cave and rubbed his chin. Leif slugged him again. Riley fell on the snow face down and moaned. The loose dog pounced and tore into a sleeve. Riley screamed in pain.

Leif yanked the dog off. With its tail between its legs, the dog crept over to a snow bank and crouched down with a watchful stare. Leif pulled off Riley's belt and bound his hands with it. "Tish, see any rope in the sled?"

Under bags and blankets, I came up with a length of rope. Leif dragged a dazed Riley onto the sled and tied him down. Leaving him there, Leif sprinted toward the cave. He stopped at the mineshaft bucket. It was a bucket made with wood slabs wired together and big enough to carry a couple of men down into the mine.

I looked at my choices of staying by the

growling dog and the bound man yelling curses, or to go down the dark hole into the cave. I hurried after Leif. "Wait for me."

Leif climbed into the mineshaft bucket and pointed at a can filled with wooden sticks. "Grab one of those torches, Tish."

I snatched a stick that had one end wrapped in burlap and was damp with smelly kerosene. I climbed over the side of the bucket. Leif released the cable and we descended into a black hole. I crouched on the floor with breath held and eyes squeezed shut. We fell swiftly. The bucket stopped with a bang that rattled through my bones. It echoed off walls of rock.

My eyes opened to a veil of blackness that smelled dank and wet. The sound of an unseen stream was heard trickling by us somewhere in the rocks.

"Leif, do you have matches?" My mitten clutched the torch.

"I hope so." I heard a click as Leif unsnapped his jacket and rustled an inside pocket.

A match scraped the rock wall. It sparked, then a tiny flame ignited the fuel-soaked torch. I handed it to Leif. He held it high above his face that glistened with beads of sweat. An orange light cast dancing shadows up jagged rocks. Leif helped me climb out of the bucket onto a narrow ledge.

"Julianne," I called. "Where are you?"

"Are you, are you," answered an echo.

"Watch your step. This ledge is narrow."

"Narrow, arrow," came Leif's echo.

Leif led the way carefully between the rock wall and moving water. The glow of the torch illuminated the tunnel only a few feet ahead of us.

"Julianne." Leif called far into the tunnel. The echo repeated her name, growing fainter little by little. We stopped and listened hard.

A weak moan pierced the dark. It came from a distance behind us. I twisted around so quickly, my foot slipped off the wet ledge. Icy water tugged on my boot with a strong current trying to suck me into the stream. I stumbled to one knee and let out a cry.

"I've got you." Leif caught on my coat and tugged me to my feet.

"Oh, thanks, Leif." I felt more of a burden than a help. "Did you hear what I heard?"

"Yes, it's got to be her. Julianne!"

Only the eerie echo answered, "Julianne, lianne, anne, anne."

I edged back along the ledge with Leif following.

"Do you see her anywhere, Tish?"

"Yes, yes. She's over there." Light from the torch flickered on a milky white face framed by the wolf ruff on her parka.

"Julianne." I fell to my knees and lifted her head. "Can you hear me?"

There was no answer. Julianne's eyes were closed. Her body lay limp.

Leif ran his fingers over her face then felt the pulse in her neck. "Let's get her out of here."

He handed me the torch. It sputtered, low on fuel. Leif lifted Julianne into his arms and inched along the narrow ledge with his back against the rock wall.

By the time Leif got Julianne settled inside the mineshaft bucket, the last ember on the torch died. In the dark, I snuggled her against me as best I could.

Leif pulled on the ropes and the bucket inched back up. The circle of outdoor light above us grew larger very slowly. What had taken us seconds to go down was long and tedious to creep back up. I wished I could help Leif pull, but there was barely space to dodge his working arms.

Julianne moaned. I squeezed her. "You'll be okay, Julianne. It's me, Tish. Leif and I will take care of you." I rubbed her icy cold fingers and tugged my mittens onto her hands.

Leif grunted as he yanked on the rope, pulling us up with all his strength. Finally, the bucket reached the light of day.

When Tim Riley saw Leif carrying Julianne, he yelled, "It weren't my fault. She fell on her own."

"I hate you!" I hollered above barking dogs.

"Hey, where you going? You can't leave me here."

"Leif is flying Julianne to the hospital."

Leif called back over his shoulder, "If you're lucky, Riley, the constable will come to your rescue before dark."

"You can't leave me tied up like this, not with these dogs. That loose one's growling at me."

"You left my sister, didn't you?" I ran after Leif.

Tim Riley shouted cuss words. The more he yelled, the more the dogs barked.

I climbed into the Jenny and Leif settled Julianne gently beside me. I pulled blankets around her.

Leif went to work outside the plane. With his own strength, he lifted and pulled on the tail, backing it up. He pushed against a wing to align the plane where tracks were formed in the snow when we landed. One pull on the propeller and the engine roared.

With the sound of the engine, Julianne's eyes fluttered open for an instant. She gave my hand a weak squeeze. I pulled on my goggles and covered her face with the parka hood.

Leif climbed into the cockpit and gunned the engine. The Jenny jogged on the snow, hitting bumps, tipping this way and that for endless seconds. Then the skis slipped over the edge of the mountain. We were airborne in a downward plunge. My stomach rose to my throat. The little plane swooped down the slope then gained enough speed to turn and soar up. It leveled off and we headed toward the valley.

Minutes dragged by like hours. Leif anxiously glanced at Julianne with eyes bloodshot behind his goggles. I thought how different he was now. I knew him always to be in control and sure of every step. Today he was like a man with cracking ice under his feet.

The sky was aflame with the setting sun

as the Jenny circled above Fairbanks. Again we were big news. People, who heard the plane, were converging on the airfield. Leif brought us onto the field in a smooth landing. As soon as the plane came to a stop, Jess and Slim were there.

"I knew no good would come from you flying off in that contraption." Slim helped me out of the Jenny. He gave me a hug before he stared aghast when Leif held Julianne in his arms. "What's happened to her?"

"We need a doctor really, really quick," I answered.

With relief, we saw Dr. Noble jogging across the field. A reporter from the *Daily News-Miner* followed with a tablet in hand and pencil behind his ear. At the sight of Julianne, the doctor waved to what looked like a hearse. It chugged onto the airfield and stopped. Leif gently placed Julianne inside.

"We'll follow you to the hospital, Leif," I called as he rode off with my sister and the doctor.

"Tish, what happened out there?" Jess asked with the news reporter eagerly standing by.

I explained everything about Tim Riley's being a murderer and how we left him tied to a dogsled on Cleary Summit. The news reporter scribbled as fast as he could.

Slim scowled and fussed at my every word. "That dang constable better get up to the mine right now so that no-good bum gets thrown in jail."

"Now that the weather warmed up, three dog teams are ready to take off. I'll go tell Constable Dole where they'll find Riley." Jess trotted back across the field. The reporter followed him.

"Tish, Tish!" Alice ran across the field with her father and Steven Mills. "Was that Julianne that I saw them put in a hearse?" Her face was contorted with dread as she threw her arms around me.

"Well, little gal, it's used for a ambulance this time," Slim said.

"Dr. Noble took Julianne to the hospital." I hurriedly repeated the whole story all over again.

Steven Mills said, "I'll go snag a dogsled ride up to Cleary Summit. After all, I do have some lawyer business with Mr. Timothy Riley."

"You're so brave, Steven," Alice cooed.

He answered Alice with a glowing smile.

"Well, I'm staying right here," Slim snapped. "If I get within five feet of that varmint, I'll strangle the life out of him with my one good hand."

Steven trotted off toward howling dog teams. Mr. Allen offered to drop Slim, Alice and me off at the hospital. "If you don't mind a buckboard, Tish, after traveling by flying machine."

"After the rides I've had today, I like horses a lot."

Alice and I squeezed together for the bouncy ride through the streets and across the bridge. The hospital was on a bank of the Chena River.

We found Leif in the hospital waiting room pacing back and forth. Before he could tell us anything, Dr. Noble came in. "Julianne's had a concussion, but a good long sleep should fix her up. I will allow you to come in to see her tomorrow."

That news was like a plunge into a cool lake on a hot day, like a lighted tree on Christmas morning, like sunshine and a rainbow after a storm. My wonderful sister was alive and well. Joy made me silly with hugs for Slim, Leif, Alice, Mr. Allen and Dr. Noble. We all wore huge smiles, yet I saw a tear nearly fall from a pilot's eyes.

CHAPTER 28

Rainbows

Dr. Noble offered to drive Slim and me home in his Maxwell sedan. Leif was glad to come with us when Slim told him dinner was waiting. Tilly had left the table spread with baked spruce hen, wild cranberry sauce, mashed potatoes, peas, and a custard pie. Leif and I ate with ravenous appetites while Slim pumped us with questions. When pie was on our plates, it was our turn to ask questions.

"What all did Hector Malone have to say?" Leif asked. "Why did he want to damage my airplane?"

"I got the whole dope on that. Hector said it was for his mamma. He wanted Stella to be proud of him. Something he wanted all his life, but never got. Said all he got for attacking Julianne on that ship was a good scoldin'."

"Getting jailed a few times didn't help endear him to his mother either, I suppose," Leif said.

"Why would he want us to crash?" I felt

Slim had the answer to every mysterious thing that has ever happened. That was just one thing that made me really love him.

"That's the quirk in it. Hector thought Leif would be by himself. He didn't know you girls were foolish enough to be in that flying machine."

"He was only after Leif?"

"I don't even know the man." Leif wagged his head, bewildered.

"Hector tells it like this. His mamma needed to get rid of competition over the wealthy widow. Stella figured getting Leif out of the picture was the only way to ever get Julianne hitched to Victor."

"Isn't that preposterous?" Leif's fork tumbled out of his hand and fell to the floor. He picked it up with cheeks turning pink.

I gave him a punch in the arm. "Well, Madame Urina is a fortune teller, Leif. So she knows lots of secrets."

Leif pushed his chair back from the table and restlessly carried dishes to the sink. "Stella Malone is also a blackmailer. She tried to get Hector to scare Julianne back to Seattle so her scheme would work."

"After all, though, the one thing she

didn't plan was for Lucky Lew to die," I said.

As if he was reading my thoughts, Slim cut another piece of creamy custard pie and plopped it on my plate. "When Lucky dropped Stella from the will, she conjured up another trick to get her hands on his money."

"Yeah, like matrimony for the widow and her son, Victor," Leif said without the sign of any smile.

"What a witch!" I cut a second piece of pie for Leif as he sat down again.

He smacked the table with a clenched fist. "She belongs in jail with her son."

Slim chuckled. "Just knowing she ain't never getting her hands on Lew's gold is real fittin' punishment for that woman."

I could not stop a few big yawns and Leif began to do the same. With full tummies, tiredness was hitting us hard. When Leif bid us good night, Slim insisted that the Ford would run fine in the warmer weather so he would drive him to his apartment. I went straight to bed for a very long sleep.

Early the next morning, I waded through snow, and ran along the road to the hospital, and delivered a bag of things to Julianne. Dr. Noble didn't allow long visits, but she was definitely awake and glad for company. On the third day she was in the hospital, I was the first one to get to her room.

"Is your headache gone yet?" I asked.

"Yes, finally, and the nausea too." She sat up on pillows fluffed by indulgent nuns. "It helped to have your Raggedy Ann with me. Thanks for bringing her, Tish." She held up the doll sewn long ago by our mother.

Sister Mary Louise appeared at the door and said with a playful wink, "Your young man is here to see you, Miss. He's coming down the hall right now." The long skirt on the nun's habit swished as she scurried from the room.

When Leif walked in, he handed Julianne a box of chocolates. "I would have brought flowers, but they're not in season."

"Like under a couple feet of snow." I joked, but neither Julianne nor Leif laughed. They seemed unaware that I was in the room. They gazed at each other as if they were alone in the world.

"Hey, Leif." I tugged on his sleeve. "Did Julianne tell you about why that loose sled dog attacked Riley?"

"We were wondering about that." He took a chair next to the bed. "Where did that dog come from?"

"Julianne says the dog's paw was bleeding from running on sharp ice. It limped and could hardly run. That crazy man cut the dog from the team and was going to shoot it."

Julianne handed the box of chocolates to me. "I insisted I needed the dog on the sled to keep me warm. He swore and brutally kicked the dog before tossing it onto the sled with me."

"See, it's no wonder the dog tried to chew Riley up. Leif, you pulled that dog off him just in time, or Riley would be full of teeth marks."

Julianne nodded. "As Riley kept drinking from his flask, he got meaner and meaner to all of the dogs. At the mine, he insisted I see the spot where his son had died."

"That horrible man just left you to die down there." I gave her a bear hug and sat on the edge of her bed.

Leif cleared his throat. "The newspaper says Constable Dole found him and did some questioning up there on the mountain. Tim Riley admitted he cut the cable on Lucky Lew's Bearcat. Said he wanted revenge for the death of his son."

"How come he blamed Lucky Lew for what happened to his son?" I pulled the lid off the chocolates and inhaled the sweet aroma.

"Wasn't it an accident?"

"Not according to Timothy Riley," Julianne said. "He blamed Lew's greed for his son's death."

"Why would he be mean to you?" I plopped a luscious, cream–filled chocolate onto my tongue.

I offered a piece to Leif, but he shook his head and picked up Julianne's hand. "That bum forced you down that mineshaft."

"He said he had to show me the tomb that greed built. Down there in the dark, his cursing echoed all around us. Like a madman he kept yelling, *Keep blasting, men. Find the rich vein*! Then he struck me. I remember no more until you carried me into the light."

"Oh, Julianne." I put my arms around her again. "That was so scary for you."

When I pulled away, Julianne's gaze was beyond me. "Landing on that mountain had to be more than a little scary. Both of you saved my life." Again, I felt like a mere shadow as Julianne reached a hand out to Leif and said softly, "Thank you."

Alice burst into the room. "Julianne, you look terrific."

I slipped off the bed and Leif shifted

aside as Alice flung herself onto Julianne. "You've been here two nights. How long is the doctor keeping you?"

"Dr. Noble says one more day and I'll be fine."

Boots thumped behind us at the doorway. Alice bounced to her feet as Slim entered the crowded room.

"Ah, Julianne, those are rosy cheeks. You had us scared spitless." The way relief brightened Slim's whiskered face made me think of how much misery and worry one man had caused us.

"We hate that mean old Tim Riley." I passed the chocolates to Alice and she took a piece.

"Well, not everyone hates him. I have the juiciest news," Alice said. "You're not going to believe it."

"We already heard Victor Malone took the train to Seward so he can catch a ship for San Francisco." Julianne said.

Slim wagged his head. "I'm guessin' with the tale his brother told, he figured you three were goners. Constable Dole was sure to pinch him as an accomplice. Saving his own sly hide meant gettin' out of town fast."

"Let Frisco beware," Leif said.

"He'll fool the whole big city with magic tricks," I said, really meaning it.

Julianne chuckled. "Those flirting eyes will find Victor plenty of victims."

Alice flung her hands in the air. "That is interesting, but so is what Steven told me just an hour ago."

"I can guess Steven has been telling you real sweet things, Alice." I gave her an exaggerated wink.

Alice's face flushed cherry pink. "It's nothing like that either. It's nothing about me or about him at all."

"Then what is it, Alice?" I handed her another candy.

"Stella Malone is now Stella Riley. She got married to Tim Riley at the jail. Isn't that unbelievable?"

"Really unbelievable," Julianne and Leif said in unison.

"Why did she do that?" I asked.

"There's only one reason that woman does anything," Slim replied. "Money. Looks like she wants her hands on what Lucky willed to Riley. Figures he don't need a penny of it when he's sittin' in jail."

"Gee whiz," I said. "If he caused Lucky Lew to die, he shouldn't get any of his money."

"That will be for a judge to decide," Leif said, shaking his head.

"It's not fair." I pouted.

"Tish and I have news too," Julianne said in a serious, hushed way. She hesitated and gave me a meaningful look.

I gave her a wink. "We had a long talk last night."

"We have made a decision about what is a right and fair way to use Lucky Lew's money."

Alice spoke up with chocolate smeared lips, "What's fair is that half of Lucky Lew's money should have always belonged to your Papa."

"Lucky Lew cheated him," I added with a sigh.

Julianne nodded in agreement. "Papa would be pleased that we decided to put a portion of it away for Tish's future."

Slim put an arm around me. "Just what have you two been cookin' up? Remember, Lucky expected every penny to stay in the Territory."

Julianne hesitated. She looked intently from one face to the next. "We plan to invest it in the future of Alaska."

"In airplanes!" I shouted. "And when I have a career, it'll be because I graduated from pilot school."

Slim slapped his leg. "You're gambling it away on those fool flying machines?"

Leif looked at Julianne with his mouth agape. His wide open eyes were bluer than the sky.

"Could Rainbow Flight Service use a couple new airplanes, Leif? We'd like to invest."

"Sure. O course, we could. We need all the help we can get." Leif clasped her hand and pressed it gently to his lips.

"Julianne, does this mean you're a professional businesswoman?" Alice asked.

"We will still need her in the office to keep us straight," Leif said.

"My sister will be there." My heart was full.

Julianne smiled broadly. "Of course, that is a perfect way to protect our investment."

"Well, every one of those big bucks were made here in Alaska, so it'll be right that it gets lost here too." Slim's grin spread across long, shaggy whiskers.

"It won't be lost," Leif said with all the confidence and spirit of a barnstormer.

"Just watch, Slim, it'll soar over rainbows." I twirled about, ready to dance.

We all laughed, including Slim.

END

ABOUT THE AUTHOR

Marie Osburn Reid loves to tell readers about Alaska in the past and present. ***OVER RAINBOW*** is a novel worked on from time to time over many years by the author. The mystery is a treat for readers as young as 13 or anyone interested in what times were like in Alaska at the beginning of the aviation era. The book is available in both paperback and e-Book for Kindle through Amazon.com.

Alaska has been the author's home ever since it was granted statehood. She is a graduate from Chico State University in California with a major in Business and a minor in English. She held several jobs through the years and is currently retired from the beloved University of Alaska Museum of the North. Her three children were born and raised in Fairbanks. She considers it a great place to live with her husband Reford (Jeep) Reid, especially in summer!

Author may be contacted on Facebook or by email at: jeep.marie@earthlink.net

PREVIOUS PUBLICATIONS

CLIMBING THE GREAT DENALI is a fiction novella based greatly on a journal kept during the second time Mitchell Austin Ward climbed Mt. McKinley. Marie Osburn Reid based the book on her son's expert mountaineer experience. He was a great help in contributing true facts for this story that is an exciting read for youths 13 or anyone older.

SPIRIT BASKET, OVER 200 YEARS OF ADVENTURES IN ALASKA is a novel for kids and adults who are curious about the history and culture of Alaska. Characters by Marie Osburn Reid come to life to tell the story. This paperback is an historical novel telling of a Native family, one generation at a time, from 1745 to 2010. Originally the novel was published in 2009, and the author is delighted to have a revised edition available in 2011 as an eBook for Kindle.

Made in the USA
Charleston, SC
08 November 2011